P9-CLJ-276

LOUISE RENNISON

KNOCKED OUT by MY NUNGA-NUNGAS

further, further confessions of
Georgia Nicolson

HARPERTEMPEST
An Imprint of HarperCollinsPublishers

Knocked Out by My Nunga-Nungas:
Further, Further Confessions of Georgia Nicolson
Copyright © 2001 by Louise Rennison
All rights reserved. No part of this book may be used or reproduced
in any manner whatsoever without written permission except in the case
of brief quotations embodied in critical articles and reviews. Printed in
the United States of America. For information address HarperCollins
Children's Books, a division of HarperCollins Publishers, 1350 Avenue of the
Americas, New York, NY 10019.
www.harperteen.com

Library of Congress Cataloging-in-Publication Data is available.
ISBN 0-06-623656-8
ISBN 0-06-623695-9 (lib. bdg.)

Typography by Alison Donalty
5 6 7 8 9 10 ❖ First HarperTempest edition, 2002
Originally published in Great Britain in 2001 by Piccadilly Press

Visit Georgia at www.georgianicolson.com

To my lovely family and fab mates. You know who you are
and it is useless to beg me not to mention you in public. Come on,
you know you are proud!!! Yes you are . . . Mutti, Vati, Kimbo,
Sophie, John, Eduardo, Honor, Libbs, Millie and Arrow, Apee,
Francesbirginia and family, Salty Dog, Jools and the Mogul, big Fat
Bob, Jimjams, Elton, Jeddbox, Phil and Ruth, Lozzer, Mrs. H, Geoff
"Oh is that champagne?" Thompson, Mizz Morgan, Alan
"It's not a perm" Davies, Roge the Dodge, Jenks the Pen, Tony the
Frock, Kim and Sandy, the fab St. Nicolas crew, Fanny Fanshawe,
Black Dog the Captain, Downie trousers, the Ace mob from
Parklands, Caroline, cock of the North and family, to the English
team of magnificence—Brenda, Jude, Emma and Clare and
Gillon. And to all the lovely, lovely Hamburger-a-gogo types who
have written to me to tell me they love my books. Thank you.
Finally a very huge ginormous thank you to the marvy
HarperCollins family and in particular to the MARVY
beyond Marvydom Alix Reid.

A Note from Georgia

Dear tiny American chums,

It is I! Georgia, your English pal, writing to you from the exciting organ that is my mind.

Here is the third part of my diary. I hope you *aime* it a lot, as much as *Angus, Thongs + FFs* and *On the Bright Side, I'm Now the Girlfriend of a Sex God*. Hey, guess what, do you know that in England the second book is called *It's OK, I'm Wearing Really Big Knickers*?

The title was changed because apparently you don't wear knickers in Hamburger-a-gogo land. At first I thought that meant that you were all in the nuddy-pants under your skirts, but no, it means that you call knickers "panties." I don't know why when they are clearly knickers. But have it your own way. At least you are not as bonkers as people in Germany. My first book there is called *Frontal Knutschen,* which is German for full-frontal snogging. Frankly I will not be *knutsch*ing anyone in Germany.

Anyway as usual in the interests of world diplomacy I have agreed to do a glossary AGAIN, in the back of this book, for words that you might not understand.

You'll laugh at this. . . . I was told that you wouldn't even know what nunga-nungas are!!!!!! I said, "They're not thick, you know, Americans, just because they don't talk properly."

Anyway, pip pip for now.

Lots of luuuuuuurve,

Georgia

P.S. You don't know what nunga-nungas are, do you?

P.P.S. Oh good grief.

P.P.P.S. You know I love you all though, don't you? Even though you are so dim.

october
return of the loonleader

thursday october 21st
my room
1:00 p.m.

Looking out of my bedroom window, counting my unblessings. Raining. A lot. It's like living fully dressed in a pond.

And I am the prisoner of whatsit.

I have to stay in my room pretending to have tummy lurgy so that Dad will not know I am an ostracized leper banned from Stalag 14 (i.e., suspended from school). I'm not alone in my room, though, because my cat, Angus, is also under house arrest for his love romps with Naomi the Burmese sex kitten.

2:00 p.m.

They'll be doing P.E. now.

I never thought the day would come when I would long to hear Miss Stamp (Sports Oberführer

and part-time lesbian) say, "Right, girls, into your P.E. knickers!"

But it has.

3:30 p.m.

All the ace gang will be thinking about the walk home from school. Applying a touch of lippy. A hint of nail polish. Maybe even mascara because it is R.E. and Miss Wilson can't even control her tragic seventies hairdo let alone a class. Rosie said she was going to test Miss Wilson's sanity by giving herself a face mask in class and seeing if Miss Wilson had a nervy spaz.

Jas will be practicing her pouting in case she bumps into Tom.

3:50 p.m.

How come Jas got off with cloakroom duty and I got banned? I am a whatsit . . . a scapethingy.

4:10 p.m.

Robbie the Sex God (MY NEW BOYFRIEND!!! Yesss and three times yesss!!!!!) will be going home now. Walking along in a Sex Goddy sort of way. A walking snogging machine.

4:30 p.m.

Mutti came in. "Right, you can start making your startling recovery now, Georgia."

Oh cheers. Thanks a lot. Good night.

Just because Elvis Attwood, school caretaker from the Planet of the Loons, tripped over his own wheelbarrow (when I told him Jas was on fire), I am banned from school.

Mutti rambled on, although she makes very little sense since Vati got home. "It's your own fault. You antagonize him and now you are paying the price."

Yeah, yeah, rave on.

4:45 p.m.

Phoned Jas.

"Jas."

"Oh hi, Gee."

"Why didn't you phone me?"

"You're phoning me. I would have got the engaged tone."

"Jas, please don't annoy me. I've only been speaking to you for two seconds."

"I'm not annoying you."

"Wrong."

"Well, I've only said about two words to you."

"That's enough."

Silence.

"Jas."

Silence.

"Jas, what are you doing?"

"I'm not annoying you."

She drives me to the brink of madnosity. Still, I really needed to speak to her so I went on, "It's really crap at home. I almost wish I hadn't been banned from school. How was Stalag fourteen? Any goss?"

"No, just the usual. Nauseating P. Green smashed a chair to smithereens and back."

"Really?! Was she fighting with it?"

"No, she was sitting on it having her lunch. It was the jumbo-sized Mars bar that did it. Everyone was killing themselves laughing. The Bummer Twins started singing 'Who ate all the pies' to her, but Slim, our beloved headmistress, heard them and gave us a lecture about mocking the unfortunate."

"Were her chins going all jelloid?"

"Yeah. In fact, it was Chin City."

"Fantastic. Are you all missing me? Did anyone talk about me or anything?"

4

"No, not really."

Charming. Jas has a lot of good qualities though, qualities you need in a bestest pal. Qualities like, for instance, going out with the brother of a Sex God. I said, "Has Hunky, I mean, Tom, mentioned anything that Robbie has said about me?"

"Erm . . . let me think."

Then there was this slurp-slurp noise.

She was making slurping noises.

"Jas, what are you eating?"

"I'm sucking my pen top so I can think better."

Sacré bloody *bleu*, I have got *le* idiot for a pal. Forty-nine centuries of pen sucking later she said, "No, he hasn't said anything."

7:00 p.m.
Why hasn't Robbie mentioned me? Hasn't he got snogging withdrawal?

8:00 p.m.
I can hear Vati singing "If I Ruled the World." Good Lord. I have only just recovered from a very bad bout of pretend lurgy. He has no consideration for others.

8:05 p.m.

The worsterosity of it is that the Loonleader (my vati) has returned from Kiwi-a-gogo land and I thought he would be there for ages. But sadly life was against me and he has returned. Not content with that, he has insisted we all go to Och Aye land to "bond" on a family holiday.

However . . . nananana and who-gives-two-short-flying-pigs'-botties? Because I live in Love Heaven.

Lalalalalala.

I am the girlfriend of a Sex God!!

8:15 p.m.

The Sex God said I should phone him when I get back from Scotland. But there is a fly in his ointment . . . I am not going to Scotland!!! My plan is this, everyone else goes to Scotland and . . . I don't! Simple enough, I think, for anyone to understand.

operation explain-brilliant-not-going-to-scotland plan to mutti and vati

8:30 p.m.

The olds were slumped in front of the TV canoodling

and drinking wine. They are so childish. I had to leave the room in the end because Dad did this really disgusting thing. They were laughing and grappling about on the sofa and they did number five on the snogging scale (open-mouth kissing). Honestly. I mean it. There might even have been a suggestion of six (tongues). Erlack a pongoes!!!! Libby was there as well. Laughing along. It can't be healthy for a toddler to be exposed to porn.

I'm sure other people's parents don't do this sort of thing. In fact, some of my mates are lucky enough to have parents that are split up. I've never really seen Jas's dad. He is usually upstairs or in his shed doing some DIY. He just appears now and again to give Jas her pocket money.

That is a proper dad.

11:00 p.m.
Before I went to bed I explained to the elderly snoggers (from outside the door just in case they were touching each other) that I will not in a zillion years be going on the family excursion to Scotland tomorrow and said good night.

friday october 22nd
scotland
raining
10:30 p.m.

I have come on holiday by mistake.

This is the gorgeous diary of my fantastic family holiday in Och Aye land. Five hundred years driving with a madman at the wheel (Dad) and another two mad things in a basket (Angus and Libby). After two hours of trying to find the cottage and listening to Vati ramble on about the "wonderful countryside," I was ready to pull his head off, steal the car and drive, drive like the wind. The fact that I can't drive stopped me, but actually I'm sure that once behind the wheel I could pick it up. How difficult can it be anyway? All Dad does is swear at other cars and put his foot down on some pedal thing.

Finally arrived at some crap cottage in the middle of nowhere. The nearest shop is twelve hundred miles away (well, a fifteen-minute walk). The only person younger than one hundred and eighty is a half-witted boy (Jock McThick) who hangs around the village on his pushbike (!)

In the end out of sheer desperadoes I went outside after supper and asked Jock McThick what him and his mates did at nights. (Even though I couldn't give two short flying sporrans.) He said, "Och." (Honestly he said that.) "We go awa' doon to Alldays, you ken." (I don't know why he called me Ken but that is the mystery of the Scottish folk.) It was like being in that film *Braveheart*. In fact, in order to inject a bit of hilariosity into an otherwise tragic situation I said when we first saw the cottage, "You can tak our lives, but you cannae tak our freedom!!"

1:15 a.m.

It's a nightmare of noise in this place, hooting, yowling, snuffling . . . and that's just Vati! No, it's the great Scottish wildlife. Bats and badgers and so on . . . Haven't they got homes to go to? Why do creatures wake up at night? Do they do it deliberately to annoy me? At least Angus is happy here, now that he is not under house arrest. It was about one A.M. before he came in and curled up in his luxurious cat headquarters (my bed).

saturday october 23rd

10:30 a.m.

Vati back as Loonleader with a vengeance. He came barging into "my" (hahahahahaha) room at pre-dawn, waggling his new beard about. I was sleeping with cucumber slices on my eyes for beautosity purposes so at first I thought I had gone blind in the night. I nearly did go blind when he ripped open my curtains and said, "Gidday, gidday, me little darlin'" in a ludicrous Kiwi-a-gogo twang.

I wonder if he has finally snapped? He was very nearly bonkers before he went to Kiwi-a-gogo land and having his shoes blown off by a rogue bore can't have helped. But hey, El Beardo is, after all, my vati and that also makes him vati of the girlfriend of a Sex God. So I said quite kindly, "*Guten morgen*, vati. Could you please go away now? Thank you."

I think his beard may have grown into his ears however, because he ignored me and opened the window. He was leaning out, breathing in and out and flapping his arms round like a loon. His bottom is not tiny. If a very small pensioner was accidentally walking along behind him they might think there had been an eclipse of the sun.

"Aahh, smell that air, Georgie. Makes you feel good to be alive, doesn't it?"

I pulled my duvet round me. "I won't be alive for much longer if that freezing air gets into my lungs."

He came and sat on the bed. Oh God, he wasn't going to hug me, was he? Fortunately Mutti yelled up the stairs, "Bob, breakfast is ready!" and he lumbered off. Breakfast is ready? Has everyone gone mad? When was the last time Mum made breakfast?

Anyway, ho hum pig's bum, I could snuggle down in my comfy holiday bed and do dreamy-dreamy about snogging the Sex God in peace now.

10:32 a.m.
Wrong.

Clank, clank. "Gergy! Gingey!! It's me!!"

Oh Blimey O'Reilly's trousers, it was Libby, mad toddler from the Planet of the Loons. When my adorable little sister came in I couldn't help noticing that although she was wearing her holiday sunglasses she wasn't wearing anything else. She was also carrying a pan. I said, "Libby, don't bring the pan into . . . "

But she ignored me and clambered up into my bed, shoving me aside to make room. She has got hefty little arms for a child of four. She said, "Move up, bad boy. Mr. Pan tired."

Then she and Mr. Pan snuggled up against me. I almost shot out of bed, her bottom was so cold . . . and sticky . . . urghh.

What is it with my room? You would think that at least on holiday I might be able to close my door and have a bit of privacy to do my holiday project (fantasy snogging), but oh no. There will probably be a coachload of German tourists in lederhosen looking round my room in a minute.

I'm going to go and find the local locksmith (Hamish McLocksmith) and get two huge bolts for my door and you can only get in by appointment.

Which I will never make.

11:00 a.m.

Libby has clanked off with Mr. Pan, thank the Lord. I don't like to be near her naked botty for long, as something always lurks out of it.

I think Mum and Dad are playing catch down-stairs. I can hear them running up and down and giggling, "Gotcha," and so on. *Sacré* bloody *bleu.*

Très pathetico. Vati's only been back for eighty-nine hours and I feel more than a touch of the sheer desperadoes coming on.

11:10 a.m.
Still, who cares about his parentosity and beardiness? Who cares about being dragged to the crappest, most freezing place known to humanity? I, Georgia Nicolson, offspring of loons, am, in fact, the GIRLFRIEND OF A SEX GOD. Yessssss!!!! Fab and treble marvelloso. I have finally trapped a Sex God. He is mine, miney, mine, mine. There is a song in my heart and do you know what it is? It is that well-known chart topper "Robbie, oh Robbie, I . . . er . . . Lobbie You!!! I Do I Do!!!"

1:00 p.m.
Hung around sitting on the gate watching the world go by. Unfortunately, it didn't. All that went by were some loons talking gibberish (Scottish) and a ferret.

Then Jock McThick or whatever his name is loomed up on his bike. He has an unfortunate similarity to Spotty Norman, i.e., acne of the head.

This is not enhanced by him being a ginger nob. Jock said, "Me and the other lads meet oop at aboot nine just ootside Alldays. Mebbe see you later."

Yeah right, see you in the next life, don't be late. Nothing is going to make me sadly go and hang out with Jock and his mates.

8:59 p.m.
Vati suggested we have a singsong round the piano tonight and started off with "New York, New York."

9:00 p.m.
I took Angus for a walk to check out the nightlife that Jock McThick told me about. Angus is the only good thing about this trip. He's really perked up. I know he longs for Naomi the sex kitten in his furry inside brain, but he is putting a brave face on it. In fact, he is strutting around like he owns Scotland. This is, after all, his birthplace. He can probably hear the call of the Scottish Highlands quite clearly here. The call that says, "Kill everything that moves." There were four voles all lined up on the doorstep this morning. Mum said she found a dead mouse in her tights. I didn't ask

where she had left them. If I ask her anything she just giggles and goes stupid. Since Dad came home her brain has fallen out.

Angus has made a new furry chum. None of the other local cats will come near our cottage. I think there was a duffing-up challenge last night. The black-and-white cat I saw in the lane yesterday has quite a bit of its ears missing now. Angus's new mate is a retired sheepdog called Arrow. I say he is retired, but sadly he is too barmy and old to know that he is retired, so he keeps rounding things up anyway. Not usually sheep though . . . things like chickens, passing cars . . . old Scottish people doing their haggis shopping. Angus hangs out with Arrow and they generally terrorize the neighborhood and lay waste to the wildlife.

9:30 p.m.
It's quite sweet and groovy walking along with Angus and Arrow. They pad along behind me. At least I have got some intelligent company in this lonely Sex Godless hellhole.

When the three of us got to Alldays, Scotland's premier nightspot, I couldn't believe it.

Alldays turns out to be a tiny twenty-four-hour supermarket.

Not a club or anything.

A bloody shop.

And all the "youth" (four Jock McThicks on bikes) just go WILD there. They hang around in the aisles in the shop, listening to the piped music! Or hang about outside on their pushbikes and go in the shop now and again to buy Coca-Cola or "Irn-bru"!

Sacré bloody *bleu* and *quel dommage*.

midnight

That was it. The premier nightspot of Scotland.

I said to Mutti, "Have you noticed how exceptionally crap it is here?"

And she said, "You have to make your own fun in places like this. You have to make things happen. Anyway, you do exaggerate."

12:30 a.m.

Hoot hoot. Scuffle scuffle. Root root. Hey, Mutti is right, it is FANTASTIC fun here!! There's an all-night party going on right outside my window!!! I would join in, but sadly I am not a badger.

sunday october 24th

10:20 a.m.

Still in Och Aye land. Tartan*trousers for as far as the eye can see.

10:31 a.m.

How many hours has it been since I saw Robbie now? Hmmm, ninety hours and thirty-six minutes.

11:00 a.m.

How many minutes is that?

11:34 a.m.

Oh God, I don't know. I can't do multiplication very well: it's too jangly for my brain. I've tried to explain this to Miss Stamp, our maths Oberführer (and part-time lesbian). It is not, as she stupidly suggests, that I am too busy writing notes to my mates or polishing my nails to concentrate. It is just that some numbers give me the mental droop.

Eight, for instance.

It's the same in German. As I pointed out to Herr Kamyer, there are too many letters in German words. The German types say *goosegott* in the morning: how normal is that? In fact, how can you take a language like that seriously? Well, you can't, which is why I only got sixty percent on my last German exam.　　　*

11:50 a.m.
I'm just going to lie in bed conserving my strength for a snogging extravaganza when I get home.

midday
Mutti came into my room with a tray of sandwiches. I said, "*Goosegott in Himmel*, Mutti, have you gone mad? Food? For me? No, no, I'll just have my usual bit of old sausage."

She still kept smiling. It was a bit eerie actually. She was all dreamy. Wafting around in a see-through nightie. Good Lord.

"Are you having a nice time, Gee? It's gorgeous here, isn't it?"

I looked at her ironically.

She raved on, "It's fun though, isn't it?"

"Mum, it's the best fun I've had since . . . er . . . since Libby dropped my makeup into the loo."

She tutted, but not even in her usual violent tutting way. Just like, nice tutting.

Even though I started reading my *Don't Sweat the Small Stuff for Teens* book she still kept raving on. About how great it was to be a "family" again. I wish she would cover herself up a bit more. Other people's mothers wear nice elegant old-peoples' wear, and she just lets her basoomas and so on poke out willy-nilly. And they certainly do poke out willy-nilly. They are GIGANTIC.

She said, "We thought we might go to the pencil-making factory this afternoon."

I didn't even bother saying anything to that.

"It will be a laugh."

"No, it won't, when did we last have a laugh as a family? Apart from when Grandad's false teeth went down that woman's bra?"

1:00 p.m.

The lovebirds went off to the pencil factory. They only got Libby to go with them because she thinks they are going to go see the pencil people. And I do mean pencil people. Not people who make pencils. Pencil people. People who are pencils. She'll go ballistic when she finds out it's just some Scottish blokes making pencils.

19

Oh, I am SO bored. Hours and hours of wasted snogging opportunities.

1:20 p.m.
I'd go out but there is nothing to look at. It just goes trees, trees, water, hill, trees, trees, Jock McTavish, Jock McTavish. What is the point of that?

On the plus side, I am going out with a SEX GOD!

1:36 p.m.
Oh *Gott in Himmel!* What is the point of going out with a Sex God if no one knows?

4:00 p.m.
I wonder if I should phone him.

4:05 p.m.
Not to speak to him as such. Just to remind him that I am his girlfriend.

4:10 p.m.
No one here knows that I am the secret girlfriend of a Sex God.

5:00 p.m.

No one at home knows I am the secret girlfriend of a Sex God.

5:15 p.m.

I am like a mirage. In a frock.

7:00 p.m.

Forced to go and sit in the pub with the elderly loons to "celebrate." Libby is being baby-sat by Jock McThick's parents. I hope they have fastened her nighttime nappy securely; otherwise their cottage will not be a poo-free zone. The pub was full of Ye Olde Scottish People (i.e., loads of loonies like my grandad, only wearing kilts). Yippeee. This is the life (not). I asked Vati for a Tía María on the rocks with just a hint of crème de menthe, but he pretended not to hear me. Typico. On the way home M and D were linked up, singing "Donald, Where's Your Trousers?" whilst I skulked along behind them. It was incredibly dark, no streetlamps or anything. As we tramped along the "grown-ups" were laughing and crashing about (and in Dad's case farting) when this awful thing happened.

I felt something touch my basooma. I thought it was the Old Man of the Loch and I leapt back like a leaping banana. Jock McThick spoke from out of the darkness, "Och, I'm sorry. I couldnae see a thing in the dark. I was just like . . . you know . . . feeling my way hame." And he scuttled off.

Hame? Why was he calling me Hame? He used to call me Ken.

11:30 p.m.
Feeling his way? Feeling his way to where? My other basooma?

This was disgusting.

11:45 p.m.
Molesting my nunga-nungas.

Nunga-nunga molester.

11:48 p.m.
Despite the incredible crapness of my life, my nunga-nungas have made me laugh. *Nunga-nungas* is what Ellen's brother and his mates call girls' basoomas. He says it is because if you pull out a girl's breast and let it go . . . it goes

nunga-nunga-nunga. He is obviously a touch on the mental side.

11:50 p.m.
But quite funny though.

11:55 p.m.
Perhaps I could make some nunga-nunga protectors by electrifying my sports bra with a battery type thing. That would give Jock McThick or any other nunga-nunga marauders a shock.

midnight
But it would also give me a shock, which is *la mouche* in the ointment.

12:10 a.m.
Angus has rediscovered his Scottish roots. Apparently they are in the middle of some bog because he had bits of horrible slimy stuff in his whiskers. He came into my bed purring and all damp and muddy. He soon got nice and dry by wiping himself on my T-shirt.

God, he smells disgusting. I think he's been

rolling in fox poo again. He thinks it's like a sort of really attractive aftershave.

1:00 a.m.
It isn't.

monday october 25th
10:10 a.m.
Why oh why oh why has the SG not called me? Oh hang on, I know why he hasn't. It's because we haven't got a phone in our fantastic cottage. I couldn't believe it when we first arrived. I said to Mutti, "There has been some mistake. I'm afraid we must go back to civilization immediately. I'll drive."

Dad raved on about "tranquility" and the simple life.

I said, "Vati, you can be as simple as you like, but I want to talk to my mates."

He grumbled on about my constant demands. As I pointed out to him, if he would buy me a mobile phone like everyone else on the planet I wouldn't have to bother speaking to him at all.

2:00 p.m.

I can't stand much more of this. The rest of my "family" has gone on a forced march. Well, Vati called it "a little walk in the woods." But I know about his little walks. It will end in tears, but this time they will not be mine. I know exactly what will happen. The Loonleader will be all bossy and "interested" in stuff like cuckoo spit. Then he'll lose the way and argue with Mutti about the right way home, fall over something and be attacked by sheep. And that will only be the high spots.

I pretended I had a headache.

Vati said to me as I lay in my pretend bed of pain, "You've probably given yourself eyestrain looking in that bloody mirror all the time."

I said, "If I develop a brain tumor you will be the first person I will come to because of your great kindness and sympathosity."

4:20 p.m.

On the edge of sheer desperadoes. Decided to go for a walk.

Arrow tried to round me up as I came out of the gate. So to make him happy I let him herd me into a hedge for a bit. Then I set off down the lane. Ho hum. Birds singing, ferrets ferretting, Jock McThicks McThicking around. Good grief. Then I came across a phone box.

A phone box!!!

A link to the real world!!! It wasn't even a tartan phone box!!

I skipped inside and dialed Jas, my very bestest mate in the universe.

"Jas, it's me!!!! God, it's good to speak to you. What's been happening???"

"Er . . . well . . . I got this fab new foundation. It's got gold bits in it that make you . . ."

It is like talking to the very, very stupid. (In fact, it IS talking to the very stupid.) I had forgotten how annoying she is. Not for long though. She rambled on, "Tom is thinking about doing Environmental Studies."

I nearly said, "Who cares." But you have to be careful with Jas because she can turn nasty if she thinks you are not interested in her. I tried to think of something to say. "Oh . . . er . . . yeah . . . the environment . . . er, that's great, erm, there's a lot of, er . . . environment here; in fact, that is all there is." Then I told her about the Jock McThick fandango. She said, "Erlack a pongoes. Did you encourage him? Maybe you gave out the wrong signals."

"Jas, I was not in the nuddy-pants."

"Well, I'm just saying, Jock must have thought he could rest his hand on your basooma. Why is that? He has never rested his hand on my basoomas, for instance."

"Jas, you are three hundred miles away. You would have to have nunga-nungas the size of France for Jock to be able to rest his hand on them."

"Yes, well . . . I'm just saying, even if I was, you know, in Och Aye land, next to Jock, well, even then, you know . . ."

"What are you rambling on about?"

"I'm just saying, this is not the first time this has happened to you, is it? There was Mark, the Big Gob. . . ."

"Yeah, but . . ."

"You say it just happened. That just out of the blue he put his hand on your basooma. No one else was there so we will never really know for sure."

"I didn't . . . it was . . ."

"Perhaps Jock has heard about your reputation. Perhaps he thinks it's alright to fondle your basoomas."

I hate Jas. I slammed the phone down. I will never be talking to her again. I don't forget things. Once my mind is made up, that is it. The friendship is finito. I would rather eat one of Libby's nighttime nappies than talk to Jas again.

She is an ex–best mate. Dead to me. Deaddy dead dead. Forever.

4:22 p.m.
Phoned Jas.

"Jas, are you suggesting I am an easy fondleree?"

"I don't know. I might be."

"What do you mean 'you might be'?"

"Well, I might be . . . but I don't know what a fondleree is."

It is like talking to the very, very backward.

I explained to her as patiently as I could. "Well, it's like dumping. If you dump someone you are the dumper. And they are the dumpee."

"What has that got to do with fondling?"

"Jas, concentrate. The verb is 'to fondle.' I fondle, you fondle, he, she, it fondles, etc. But I am the recipient of the fondle, so that makes me the fondleree."

She wasn't really concentrating though. She was probably looking at herself in the mirror they have in their hall . . . imagining she is Claudia Schiffer. Just because some absolute prat told her she looked a bit like Claudia. Yeah. Claudia with a stupid fringe.

Walked back to Crap Cottage.

in my room
6:00 p.m.
Brilliant. Miles away from civilization and my so-called mate says I am an easy fondleree. Still, she is mad as a badger; everyone knows that.

9:00 p.m.
Sitting around in the tartan lounge in Crap Cottage. My breasts are making me a mockery of a sham. They are like two sticky-out beacons attracting all the sadsacks in the universe.

11:00 p.m.

Mutti came into my bedroom to get Libby out of my wardrobe. She's made a sort of nest in there that she says is a treehouse.

Over the shouting and biting I said to Mutti, "Do you think you could ask Dad if you and he could club together to let me have some money for breast reduction surgery?"

It took her about a year to stop laughing.

It's pointless asking for money. I can't even get a fiver out of Dad for some decent lip gloss. He would never give me the money. Even if my breasts were so big that I had to have two servants called Carlos and Juan to carry them around for me.

tuesday october 26th

10:00 a.m.

The postman came this morning. He didn't have any post, he just said, "Good morning to ye. It's nice to have a good-looking lassie round the place."

He was quite groovy-looking. A bit like a young Sean Connery. But with more hair on his head. And quite nice lips.

10:15 a.m.

Oh Blimey O'Reilly's pantaloons, I think I have got general snoggosity syndrome.

11:00 a.m.

Maybe Jas is right. I have become an easy fondleree because of my pent-up snogging deprivation.

Oh Robbie, where are you now? Rescue me from this valley of the loons.

4:29 p.m.

Accidentally found myself next to the phone box.

Uh-oh. Temptation.

The phone box was saying to me, "Come in and use me. You know you want to."

I have been practicing maturiosity by not phoning the Sex God. It seems like a lifetime since he last snogged me. My lips have definitely got snog withdrawal. I found myself trying out kissing techniques on scuba-diving Barbie last night. Which is truly sad. I must pass by the phone box with complete determinosity.

4:30 p.m.

Brring brring.

Please don't let it be Robbie's mum or dad. Please don't let me have to be normal. Oh thank goodness SG answered the phone. Jellyknickers all round.

He said "Hello" in a Sex Goddy sort of a way. Wow!!

Then he said "Hello" again.

Wow.

Then I realized that normally when you phone someone up you are supposed to say something. And that something is NOT "I love you, I love you" or "Ngyunghf." So I took the bullet by the horns and said, "Hi . . . Robbie . . . it's me. Georgia." (Very good, I had even said the right name!!!) He sounded like he was really pleased to hear from me. "Gee! How are you, gorgeous?"

Gorgeous. He, me called, gorgeous. Me, I. Georgia to brain! Georgia to brain! Shut up shut up shut up!!!!!

He said, "Gee, are you there? Are you having a good time?"

"Fantastic, if you like being bored beyond the Valley of Boredom and into the Universe of the Very Dull."

He laughed. (Hurrah!!!) Oh, it was so dreamy

to talk to him. I told him about everything. (Well, apart from being molested by Jock McThick.) He says some talent scouts are coming to see the next Stiff Dylans gig on November 6th at the Buddha Lounge!! My first official outing as an OG (official girlfriend). What shall I wear, what shall I wear? I noticed he hadn't really said anything for a bit whilst I had been rummaging through my mental wardrobe. He was not *le official grand bouche* like some people (Jas). I thought I would entertain him with an intelligent story, but all I could think of telling him about was my nunga-nunga protectors idea. Just in the knickers of time I didn't. Why couldn't I be normal with him?

Fortunately he said something. "Look, Gee, I'm really sorry but I have to go. I could talk to you all day, but I have to go off to a rehearsal. I'm late now."

Ho hum. Well I suppose this is the price I must pay for being the GIRLFRIEND OF A SEX GOD POPSTAR!!! YESSS!!!

He said, in his groovy voice full of gorgeosity, "See you later. I'd like to snog you to within an inch of your life. I'll phone you when you get back."

Ooohhhhhh.

After he had put the phone down I stroked my T-shirt with the receiver pretending it was him. But then I saw that Jock McTavish was waiting outside the telephone box looking at me, so I had to pretend I was cleaning the receiver.

5:00 p.m.
Phew.

To make Jock go away, I have said I will go to Alldays later. Which I will not. Jock seemed to believe me because he said, "Awa the noo hoots akimbo" or something.

9:00 p.m.
How soon can I get them to set off for home tomorrow? If we set off at dawn we could be back in Normal Land by about four P.M.

9:30 p.m.
I wonder if the ace gang might arrange a surprise welcome home party for me. It's half term now, so I am no longer an ostracized leper on my own. So ha-di-haha. She who laughs the last laughs, erm, a lot. Slim thought she was banning me for a week but she was banning me for two weeks!!!

10:00 p.m.

In "my" bed, with the usual crowd. Libby and the entire contents of her traveling toybox: scuba-diving Barbie, one-eyed Teddy, Pantalitzer, Panda the Punk (Libby shaved his head). The only difference is that to celebrate our holiday in Tartan-a-gogo Libby has replaced Charlie Horse with Jimmy. Jimmy is a haggis with a scarf on. Don't even ask. Libby made him this afternoon and she "lobes" him.

I am sleeping in a bed with a stuffed sheep's stomach. With a scarf on.

wednesday october 27th
6:00 a.m.

Up and packed. I tried to get Mutti and Vati to get up and make an early start, but when I went into their bedroom Vati threw his slipper at me.

9:00 a.m.

At last! Escape!!!! Soon I will be back in the arms of my Sex God. At last, at last. Thank the Lord!!! I love you, Jesus, really, really I do. Good-bye Och Aye land!!! I sat in the back of the car daydreaming of my return as OG. But as they say, "Every silver cloud has a dark lining," because Vati decided to wear his ridiculous souvenir bagpipe hat as we eventually got into the loonmobile. I got down as low as I could in the back of the car so that no one would see me. I wish I could have an inflatable dad, like in that old film *Airplane!* where there is an inflatable pilot. Still, with a bit of luck I need never see him again when I get my freedom back. Arrow looked all mournfully at Angus when we left. He will miss his furry partner in crime. Angus and Arrow, *los dos amigos bonkeros.* Angus didn't even look back. He just shot into the car and started wrestling with the car rug.

11:00 a.m.
Meanwhile in my fabulous life, another eighty-five years of my parents' company in the car going home.

Libby has insisted on bringing Jimmy the haggis home with us.

1:00 p.m.
Oh good grief. Angus ate half of Jimmy when Libby had to be taken to the piddly diddly department

at the service station. She went ballisticisimus when she found out. She hit Angus over the head with scuba-diving Barbie. I don't think he even noticed—well, he didn't stop purring. I nodded off for the whole of the Midlands because Dad started telling us about his hopes for the future. When I woke up I noticed that both Libby and Angus were nibbling away at Jimmy.

They are disgusting.

I sooooo hope that Robbie rings when I get home.

6:00 p.m.
Home!!!! Oh, thank you, thank you, Baby Jesus. I am SOOOO happy. I will never complain about my dear little home again.

6:15 p.m.
God, it's so boring here. Nothing is happening.

6:30 p.m.
No phone calls.

All my so-called mates forgot to remember that I am not dead. Don't they even wonder where I have been for the last five days?

7:55 p.m.

Jas, Jools, Ellen, Rosie, Mabs and Soph are ALL out. They've all gone to the cinema together. The Fab Gang but without one of the fab. People can be so self-obsessed. Right, well, I am going to eat the souvenirs that I brought back from Och Aye land for them.

8:25 p.m.

Lying down.

Urgh, I feel sick. I may never eat Ye Olde Short-breaddy again as long as I live.

9:00 p.m.

Tucked up in bed. I have made a barrier with my bedside table so that no one can get in my room.

Now I really have got snogging withdrawal BADLY!!

9:05 p.m.

I must see him. I must.

10:00 p.m.

Undid my barricade and went downstairs. I am so restless.

Angus is driving everyone insane!!! He is not allowed out at night until he learns his lesson vis-à-vis Naomi the sex kitten. He has to be kept away from her; otherwise he is in for the big chop. Although I would like to see the vet that could do the job and still have both arms.

Angus keeps yowling and scratching at the door. He is supposed to go to the piddly diddly department and poo parlor division in the laundry room. But he won't go in. He just hangs round the front door trying to get out, whining and scratching and occasionally licking his bottom.

Libby said, "C'mon, big pussy, I'll show you," and went and had a piddly diddly on his tray. Oh marvelous. Now we'll never get her to go to the ordinary piddly diddly department. She'll want her own tray.

Then Vati, Loonleader of the Universe, took over. "I'll deal with the bloody thing!" He dragged Angus into the laundry to put him on the cat tray. It took him about half an hour, even using the spade. Anyway, he got him in there at last. There was a lot of yowling and swearing and Vati came out two minutes later covered in kitty litter. Like the Abominable Ashtray! Even his beard was gray.

10:30 p.m.

In the end, after Angus had laid waste to four loo rolls, I was made to take him out on his lead to see if it would calm him down. God, he's strong! I mean, normally I have very little control over him, but his love has given him the strength of ten mad cats. When we got out of the door he just took off with me on the end of the lead. Straight to Naomi's love parlor. At Mr. and Mrs. Across the Road's place there was a reinforced fence round the garden, but you could see the house and there was Naomi!! The sex kitten. Languishing in the kitchen window. On the windowsill. Looking all longing. She was like me. All puckered up and nowhere to go. Poor furry thing. Angus yowled and started doing this weird shivering thing. When Naomi saw Angus she immediately lay on her back with her girlie parts flowing free. She's a dreadful minx. No wonder Angus is a wreck, driven mad by her Burmese sex kitteny charms. Still, that is male and female for you. Sex God is probably at home even now thinking about me and shivering with excitement like Angus.

10:40 p.m.

But hopefully not rubbing his bottom against a dustbin.

10:50 p.m.

We would have been there all night, but fortunately Mr. Across the Road drew the curtains and I found a bit of old sausage and managed to get Angus to trail after it. He was so miserable that I didn't lock him in the kitchen. I let him sleep on my bed even though it is strictly verboten.

I said to him very seriously, "Angus, you are on best behavior. Just lie down and go to sleep." He was all purry and friendly and licky. You see, that's all he needs—a bit of understanding.

Aahhh. It's nice having a loyal furry pal. He's a lot more loyal than some I could name but won't.

Jas.

10:55 p.m.

And Rosie, Jools, Ellen.

11:00 p.m.

Night night, Sex God, wherever you are.

midnight

Vati just went ballisticisimus. Raving on and shouting, "That is IT, that is IT!!!"

Mutti was saying, "Bob, Bob . . . put the knife down."

Has he finally snapped and will have to go to a vatihome?

12:15 a.m.

Angus has pooed in Vati's tie drawer! Hilarious, really.

El Beardo as usual did not see the joke. He dragged Angus, who was spitting at him, into the kitchen and locked him in there. Then he shouted at me, "Right, that's IT! I'm going to the vet's."

I said, "Why? Are you feeling a bit peaky?" But he didn't get it.

thursday october 28th
10:00 a.m.

Vati said to me over our marvelous breakfast of . . . er . . . nothing, "He's going to the vet's and having his chimney swept as soon as I can make an appointment."

What in the name of Sir Julie Andrews is he talking about now?

11:00 a.m.

I've got much too much on my mind to worry about chimneys. I think I may have a lurker coming on. Emergency, emergency.

11:15 a.m.

Also the orangutan gene is rearing its ugly head again. My eyebrows are so hairy they are now approaching the "It's a mustache! It's a hedge-hog!!! No, no, it's GEORGIA'S EYEBROWS!!" stage.

It doesn't even stop at the head, this rogue hair business. I've just inspected my legs. I look like I have got hairy trousers on. Dad's razor is lying there calling to me, "Come on, use me. Just a few little strokes and you could look almost human." But no, no, I must resist after what happened last time. My eyebrows took a thousand years to grow back after I accidentally shaved them off.

Hmm, but maybe Mum's hair removing cream? Just a little dab here and there.

midday

Mutti asked me if I wanted to go tenpin bowling with them! Honestly! She and Vati went off with Libby skipping along. I think M and D were holding hands. Sweet really, I suppose. I just wish it didn't make me feel so sick.

12:30 p.m.

Jas came round AT LAST. I was a bit miffed with her about last night and not bothering to come round earlier. She didn't notice, of course. She just bent over to pick up my makeup bag. I could see her vast pantibus lurking under her skirt. I said, "Jas, do you mind? I'm not feeling very well. I think I might have jet lag from coming from Och Aye land."

"You haven't got a tan."

What is the point? I gave her my worst look but she just went on using my mascara. She CANNOT stop pouting every time she sees herself in a mirror. She said, "We had a great time at the pictures. Dave the Laugh is really . . . you know . . . (pouty pout) . . ."

"What?"

"Well, you know (pouty pout) . . . a laugh."

I tried not to be sarcastic or raise my eyebrows ironically, because I didn't want to draw any attention to them. I have not quite achieved the sophisticated look that I wanted with Mum's hair remover. In fact I have achieved the someone-has-just-stuck-a-firework-up-my-bottom look. But you can't really tell unless you pull my fringe back.

Anyway, you'd have to be on fire for Jas to notice anything. She was rambling on. "Do you think I should get my hair cut really short at the back and kind of longer at the front?"

I hadn't the remotest interest in Jas's head, but I know you have to let her rave on about herself a bit, otherwise you never get to talk about yourself. Then she said, "Ellen really likes Dave the Laugh."

I thought, Oh does she really? How patheti-cosimus. Ellen my so-called mate likes my castoff Red Herring. She is like a lurking piranha fish in a skirt.

But live and let live I say. OGs display pride and general sophisticosity at all times. Jas was unaware of my sophisticosity and went looning on. "She stayed round at my place for the night and we talked until about four A.M. That's why I am so tired."

"It's nice that you have got a new lezzie mate, Jas, but what has that got to do with me?"

"She didn't sleep in my bed."

"So you say."

"Well, she didn't."

"It's nothing to be ashamed of, Jas. If you swing both ways that is your personal choice. I'm sure Tom will understand if you tell him you are a bisexual."

"Oh shut up—you're being all moody and stressy because Robbie hasn't phoned you."

She was right actually, which is annoying. I feel all pent up, like in *Cell Block H*. I said, "Let's put some really loud CDs on and go dance crazy."

We did this fab dance routine. It was duo head shaking, kick turn, jump on bed, snog teddy, then back to the head shaking. I was feeling quite perked up. Then, of course, someone had to spoil it. I had forgotten about the Return of the Mad Bearded One. He came in the front door and it was stomp, stomp, "Bloody hell!", then crash, stomp, stomp, yell. "Georgia!!! Are you deaf?!!! Turn that racket down, I could hear it at the end of the bloody street!!"

I shouted back, "Pardon? Can you speak up, Dad, there's really loud music playing!!!"

Which made Jas and me laugh a lot. But not El Beardo.

4:00 p.m.
Jas, my so-called best mate, had to go because she was doing her homework. How sad is that? Very, very sad. Also, she was doing it with her boyfriend Hunky. Hell will freeze over and become a skating rink for the mad before I will do my homework with Robbie. Sex Gods and their girl-friends do not "do homework." Life is too short.

I tried to explain the tragedy of what she was doing, but Jas just said, "I want to do well in my German exam." I laughed. But she was serious.

I said, "It is so naff to do well in German, Jas."

Jas went all huffy. "You only say that because you can't do it."

"Oh, that is so *nicht* true, Jas. *Ich bin ein guten* German speaker."

But old swotty knickers went off anyway. Hmmm.

5:00 p.m.
Swiss Family Robinson have gone to the cinema together now. It's just fun fun fun, all the way for them.

All aloney. On my owney. It's bloody nippy noodles as well. What a life. I have been back a whole day and a night and he has not called me. Why oh why oh why?

I am so fed up.

5:10 p.m.

I might as well go to bed and grow my lurker.

5:20 p.m.

Phone rang. Probably Jas asking me something about her homework. I said, *"Jahwohl!"*

5:22 p.m.

The Sex God wants me to go round to his house!!! His parents are out.

I am so HAPPY!!!

5:30 p.m.

I changed into my jeans and quickly got made up. I went for the natural look (lip gloss, eyeliner, mascara and blusher) with a touch of panstick on the lurker. You could only see the lurking lurker if you looked up my nostril, and what fool was going to do that?

But as I was going out of my bedroom door I remembered my nungas. Perhaps I should take some precautions to keep them under strict control. Maybe bits of Sellotape on the ends of them to keep them from doing anything alarming? I'd like to trust them, but they are very unreliable. Sometimes they act like they have lives of their own. One day I will look down and they will have gone out to some nunga-nunga party by themselves. Oh, oh, I have early signs of absent brain coming on!!!

outside robbie's house
6:00 p.m.

I walked through the gate, breathing the atmosphere of Sex Goddiness, and knocked on the door. My heart was beating really loudly. The door opened.

The Sex God.

Himself.

In person.

In his gorgeous black jeans and thingy top. And his dreamy army things and gorgey leggy whatsits and mouthy thing and so on. He is SO dreamy. Every time I see him it's a shock. He smiled at me. "Georgia . . . how are you?"

Excellent question. Excellent. Good. I knew the answer as well. That was the marvelous thing. I knew the answer was "Great, how are you?" Unfortunately, all the blood in my brain had gone for a bit of a holiday into my cheeks. I had a very, very red face and a completely empty brain. I couldn't speak; all I could do was be very, very red.

He just looked at me, and he smiled this really beautiful smile, all curly round the teeth. Like he really liked me. Yuuummy scrumbos.

Then he pulled me into the house and shut the door behind me. I just stood there trying not to be red. He put his arms round me and gave me a little soft kiss on the mouth, no tongues (number three on the snogging scale). But my mouth had gone into pucker mode so when he stopped my mouth was a bit behind and still a bit open. I hoped I didn't look like a startled goldfish.

He kissed me again, this time harder and longer. His mouth was all warm and wet (not wet like whelk boy though). He put one of his hands on the back of my head, which was just as well as I thought my head might fall off. And then he started kissing my neck. Little sucky kisses right up to my ear. Fanbloodytastic. After a bit of that, and believe me I could have gone on doing that for years, he put his tongue ever so softly into my ear!! Really! Ear snogging!!! Fantastic.

I think I might have lost the use of my legs then because I fell over onto the sofa. However, I quickly leapt to my feet in a gazelle(ish) sort of way. I thought I would say something normal so that he would be fooled into thinking I was normal. I said, "Did you finish your demo-disc-type-thingymedendums?"

(Yes—very nearly English!! Good, good, keep it up!!)

He smiled at me and then went and put his demo disc on. It was very groovy, but I didn't know what to do with my face. Smile? Look dreamy? Hum? Nod along to the beat? In the end, I went for gazing out of the window and tapping my foot a bit. He came and stood behind me and put his hands on my waist.

So I turned around for more snogging.

bedroom

10:00 p.m.

I am in Love Heaven. What a mega fab day. He is the Sex God of the Universe and beyond.

I crept downstairs and phoned Jas. "Jas," I whispered.

"Why are you whispering?"

"Because M and D are in the front room, and I don't want them to know I am calling you."

"Oh."

"I have had the most amazing time, I—"

"Well, I haven't, I just can't decide whether to have my hair cut for the gig. . . . Do you think yes or no? I mean, it's nice to have it long but then it's nice to have it short, but then . . ."

"Jas, Jas . . . it is my turn to talk."

"How do you know?"

"I just do."

"Oh."

"Ask me what I have just done."

"Why? Don't you know?" And she started laughing.

I forgot I was supposed to be whispering and yelled down the phone, "Jas!!!" Then I told her. "I went round to Robbie's house to see him."

Jas said, "No!"

"Mais oui!"

"Sacré bleu."

"Aujourd'hui."

"Well, what happened?"

And I said, "Well, it was beyond marvy. We talked and snogged and then he made me a sandwich and we snogged and then he played me one of his tracks and then we snogged."

"So it was like . . ."

"Yeah . . . a snogging fest."

"Sacré bleu!" Jas sounded like she was thinking which is a) unusual and b) scary.

I went on, "Yes, and guess what?"

"What?"

"He put his tongue in my ear."

"Crikey. Did it . . . couldn't it . . . accidentally . . . like stick in your brain?"

Honestly, you would get more sense out of a potato. I ignored her obvious bonkerosity and went on, "But then this weird thing happened. He was playing me his demo CD and standing behind me with his hands on my waist."

"Ooer."

"D'accord. Anyway, I turned round and he sort of leapt out of the way like two short leaping things."

"Was he dancing?"

"No . . . I think he was frightened of being knocked out by my nunga-nungas."

Then we both laughed like loons on loon tablets (i.e., a LOT).

bedroom
10:21 p.m.
Vati made me get off the phone and gave his famous We-are-not-made-of-money speech, first given in 1846.

11:00 p.m.
Emergency snogging scale update:

(1) holding hands
(2) arm around
(3) good-night kiss
(4) kiss lasting over three minutes without a breath
(5) open-mouth kissing
(6) tongues
(6½) ear snogging
(7) upper body fondling—outdoors
(8) upper body fondling—indoors (in bed)
(9) below waist activity (b.w.a.)
(10) the full monty

friday october 29th

9:58 a.m.

Dreamt of Robbie feeding me chocolate sandwiches. Which was really cool. But then he started
nibbling my ears in a sort of peckish way, and he
nibbled them both off. Then for some reason we
were in the south of France at some big gig and it
was really sunny and I got my shades out to put on
and they just fell off because I had no ears to balance them on.

I don't know what this means. Probably it
means I am feverish with love.

Very nippy noodles again. Brrrr. Oh, it snowed
during the night, that's why. When I got out of
bed and stood in the cold air my nipples did that
sticking-out thing again. On the whole I seem to
have very little control over my body.

Still, so what!!!

6:00 p.m.

Spent the day in a love haze punctuated by rescu-
ing bits of my underwear from Angus's basket. He
is in an awful mood. He climbed up the curtains
like a Tyrolean mountaineer in a furry suit. If he

was a human he would go down to the gym and work out his frustration by hitting something. Or jogging. I know how he feels.

9:00 p.m.
I tried to encourage Angus to go cat jogging. He didn't get it though. When I set off jogging he trotted along quite nicely on his lead. For about a minute. Then he got bored. He ran round and round me like a mad loon until his lead was wrapped round my ankles and all I could do was fall over into a thorn bush.

9:30 p.m.
Phone rang. OhmyGod. I almost ripped it off the wall.

It was Rosie checking arrangements for tomorrow. I could hardly hear her because there was such loud music in the background. She said, "Greetings, Earth creature . . . SVEN!!!!! You adorable Norwegian fool, turn the music down!!"

I heard laughing and stamping and then the music went quieter. Rosie said, "Jas said you did ear snogging yesterday."

Oh, thank you, Radio Jas.

saturday october 30th

9:30 a.m.

Phoned Jas for gang discussion. Where we should all meet today and so on. When she answered I came over a bit French. (Because I am in *Le* Luurve Heaven.) "*Bonjour*, Jas, it is *moi, ta grande amie.*"

"*Ah, bonjour.*"

"*Ah, d'accord*, I have just *mang*ed my breakfast; I *mang*ed the *delicieusement* toast and *le coffee de* Monsieur Nescafè."

"*Magnifique.*"

"*De rigeur.*"

We are meeting at gang headquarters (Luigi's Cafe) at one o'clock and then going for a bit of heavy makeup trying-on in Boots, etc. I have only got a measly five pounds to spend. I hope Dad manages to persuade some poor fool to give him a job soon because I am running out of lip gloss.

11:00 a.m.

Bloody hell. You take your life in your hands going into the kitchen for a snack. Angus is in there and he is not pleased. I had to fend him off with a frying pan to get into the fridge.

Still, lalalalalala.

midday

Still in a European mood, I dressed French casual (same as sports casual—black Capri pants, black rollneck top, ankle boots—but with a lot more eyeliner). In fact, the combination of Frenchosity and my snogging extravaganza made me come over all forgiving and relaxed. I even waved to Mr. Next Door as I went down the road. Typically, he just tutted. But hey ho, tut on. Nothing can spoil my mood. Mr. Next Door was wearing an extraordinary pair of trousers; they seem to start under his armpits and be made out of elephant. He said, "I hope you are keeping that wild animal under lock and key. It's about time something was done with it."

Nobody can take a joke around here. Alright, Mr. Across the Road does have a point in that Angus did abscond with Naomi, but what does Old Elephant Trousers have to complain about?

What they both fail to see are Angus's very good qualities. He has many attractive cat qualities. For instance, he has EXCELLENT balance. Only last month he herded Snowy and Whitey, Mr. Next Door's Prat Poodles, into the manure heap and then leapt down from the wall and had a ride round on Snowy's back. Like Snowy was a little horsey.

How many cats can do that?

12:30 p.m.
While I was waiting at the bus stop for a bus to town, two blokes in cars hooted their horns at me (ooer). I really have become a boy magnet.

Then along came Mark Big Gob who I unfortunately made the mistake of going out with in my youth. Well, ten months ago, anyway. He was messing about with his rough mates waiting for the bus. No sign of his midget girlfriend. Perhaps he had mislaid her. His mouth is sooo big; how could I have snogged him? And he had rested his hand on my basooma. Still, let bygones be bygones. My basoomas are out of his hands now. I am, after all, the girlfriend of a Sex God and Mark is the boyfriend of some toddler. I smiled kindly at him, and that is when he said to me, "You want to be careful not to move too quickly, Georgia. You'll have someone's eye out with those."

And he meant my nunga-nungas! And all his mates laughed.

I stood there in a dignity-at-all-times sort of way until the bus came. I sat as far away from the BG and his rough mates as I could.

12:45 p.m.
It was a relief to get off the bus. As I got off I had to go past Mark and his mates. I made sure my nungas were not making a guest appearance by hunching my shoulders over.

12:50 p.m.
I've just seen a reflection of myself in a shop window looking like the hunchback of Notre Dame in Capri pants.

1:00 p.m.
In the cafe I met up with Rosie, Ellen, Mabs, Jools and Jas. Yesssssssss! The ace gang together again!! The girls are back in town, the girls are back in town!!! We had loads of really important things to talk about: makeup, snogging and, of course, berets. This term is not going so well on the beret front. Even the lunchpack beret has lost its charm.

Rosie said, "I walked by Miss Stamp with two oranges and a banana stuck under my beret and she just raised her eyes. Something must be done."

I had a flash of total whatsit . . . wisdomosity. "*Mes* huge *amies*, I have given this seconds of thought, and I know what the answer is."

They were all agog as two gogs. Jools said, "What?"

I brought out my gloves and beret from my rucky. *"Voilà."*

They looked at me. Honestly, it was like talking to the terminally deaf.

I said again, "*Voilà* . . . glove animal!!"

Rosie said, "What in the name of Slim's gigantic knickers are you talking about?"

Good grief. It is very tiring being the girlfriend of a Sex God and a genius at the same time. "Glove animal!!! A way of dressing sensibly and snugly using both beret and gloves. You pin a glove over each ear so that it hangs down like big dog ears and then you pop the beret over the top." I clipped my gloves over my ears and popped the beret over the top (risking my hair's bounceability factor).

"*Voilà,* glove animal!!!"

Magnifique, I think everyone will agree.

8:00 p.m.

Home again To my lovely delicious supper of . . . er . . .

Mutti and Vati and Loonsister out AGAIN. Still. In Love Heaven you are never really alone.

Angus is tied up to the kitchen table leg. I gave him a hug to cheer him up, and he lashed out at me. Also I notice that he has a pair of Vati's Y-fronts in his basket. Good grief. He has gone beyond sheer desperadoes. He is really sad without Naomi. I know how he feels. Every minute without the Sex God seems about sixty seconds long.

11:30 p.m.

Halloween tomorrow.

It's impossible to sleep in my bed with Libby's pumpkin lantern in here. I suppose I should be pleased she hasn't insisted on having her witch's broom and . . .

"Libby, no, not the broom and . . ."

"Move over, bad boy."

sunday october 31st
halloween

I immediately annoyed Dad this morning by pretending that he was wearing a scary Halloween costume. In fact, his leisure slacks and Marks and Spencer's cardigan ARE very scary, but he didn't get it.

Libby is in toddler heaven because some of her little mates from kindy are coming across this afty for apple bobbing and lanterns and stuff.

11:00 a.m.

In a rare moment of sanity Vati has been over to see Mr. and Mrs. Across the Road and pleaded for Angus's manhood. He was all pleased with himself when he came back.

"I thought I'd take a look at that garden fence, Connie, see if we can keep Angus in a bit more. Then he might not have to have his biscuits nibbled."

Biscuits nibbled? What planet does he live on?

He started rooting around in the toolbox. I wish he would get a job and then he wouldn't be interested in DIY anymore. Mum said, "Bob, I beg you, please get someone competent to do the fence. You're only just back on your feet again."

Vati got all dadish. "Connie, I can fix a fence, you know."

We laughed. I helped Mum out. "Dad, there was the unfortunate leg-through-the-ceiling incident when you last went into the loft."

"There was a weakness in the roof."

"Yes, Dad, that was you."

"Don't be so bloody cheeky."

I am not wrong, though. The electrician who came to look at the fridge that blew up after Dad had "fixed it" accused Dad of being a madman. But grown-ups will never be told anything until it is too late. That is the sadnosity of grown-ups.

As Vati went into the cupboard under the stairs Mum looked at me, but what was I supposed to do? It's her husband; she should stop him. He came out of the cupboard with a hammer and a saw. I said, "Well, probably catch up with you later in Casualty then, Dad."

He swore in a very unpleasant way.

2:00 p.m.

Dad built a hilarious fence. It was sort of leany and falling-downy at the same time. It was supposed to keep Angus away from Naomi, but when

Dad was hammering in the final nail he said, "Yes, well, that should keep him safely in," and the whole fence fell over. And Angus just walked straight over the fence into Next Door's garden.

3:00 p.m.
Vati is having to pretend to be normal because Libby's kindy mates have arrived. Libby's an awfully rough hostess. When Millie and Oscar were bobbing for apples she "helped" them by banging them on the heads with her pumpkin lantern. Oscar couldn't walk straight for ages and Millie wanted to go home. Well, actually, all of the children wanted to go home.

5:30 p.m.
Angus is having a huge laugh. He keeps appearing on the top of fences and so on. He ate Snowy's play Bonio. Mr. Next Door said he will have to get a dog psychiatrist in.

Vati's been raving on and on. Outside I could see Mr. and Mrs. Next Door and Mr. and Mrs. Across the Road all muttering together and poking about with sticks. They are probably forming a lynch mob. For heaven's sake.

Vati said, "As soon as we find him, that is it—he has his trombone polished once and for all."

As Dad was grumping around, moaning on and on and banging things about in the kitchen, I said to Mum, "Will you tell Vati that I don't want to discuss things of a personal nature with him, but if he takes Angus to the vet and has his, you know, trouser snake addendums tampered with, he is no longer my vati. I will be vatiless."

Mutti just went tutting off into a world of her own.

Angus is a king amongst cats. He walks tall with his trouser snake addendums proudly dangling. Naomi is yowling all the time. Why don't they just let them be together?

november
away laughing on a fast camel

monday november 1st
at "breakfast"
7:50 a.m.

Back to school.

Sacré bleu, merde and double poo.

Angus is on his lead, yowling, tied to the kitchen table. It's like having a police car in the kitchen. He was brought back under armed guard this morning. The lynch mob only managed to get him because he tried to get in through Mr. Across the Road's catflap. To see his beloved sex kitten. No one seems to appreciate the romance of the situation. Angus had even taken Naomi a midnight snack of half-chewed haddock fillet. How romantic is that?

Vati has got a job interview this morning. With my luck he'll turn up serving hot dogs in a van outside school. With, as a *coup d'état*, Uncle Eddie as his assistant. Anyway, it means that Angus lives to polish his trombone another day.

Vati gave me a kiss on the head as he left!! Erlack!! I've asked him to respect my personal space. Well, I said, "Please don't touch me as I don't want to be sick down my school uniform."

I made for the door before anyone else could kiss me—I had seen the state of Libby's mouth after her cornflakes and Jammy Dodger. As I went through the door Angus made a desperate bid for freedom. He was fastened to the kitchen table leg, but that didn't stop him. He dragged the table along with him. It really made me laugh, because one minute Mum was eating her cornies on the table and the next minute the table and cornies were gone.

8:15 a.m.

Slouch slouch.

I saw Jas outside her gate. She was turning her skirt over at the top to make it short for the walk to school. We unroll as we approach Stalag 14 because of the ferret on guard there (Hawkeye). She lurks around the school gates like a lurking lurker. Hawkeye's life ambition is to give us bad conduct marks for breaking useless school rules. That's how fabulous her life is.

Anyway, I crept up behind Jas and yelled, *"Bonjour, sex bombe!!!"* and she nearly had a nervy spaz. Which was very funny.

I wasn't looking forward to facing *le* music. This was my first day back since I had been unjustly banned from school because Elvis Attwood had carelessly tripped over his wheelbarrow and injured himself. OK, he was chasing me at the time but . . .

When we reached the school gates I was so overcome with ennui and general pooiness that I forgot to do anything with my beret. Even Jas noticed. She said, "Gee, you've got your beret on properly."

"That is because for the time being the party is over, Jas. You may also notice that I am not wearing lip gloss."

"Crikey."

As I slinked through the gate to Nazi headquarters Hawkeye was there like an eagle in heat. She hates me. I don't know why. I am vicitimized by her. That is the sadness of my life.

As I went by her she said, "Walk properly!"

What does that mean, *Walk properly*? As an amusing example of my hilariosity, I did a bit of a limp. Hawkeye shouted after me, "Georgia, don't earn yourself a reprimand before you even get your coat off!! As soon as assembly is over report to Miss Simpson's office."

She is such a stiff! I said to Jas, "I bet she irons her knickers."

Jas started to say "What is so wrong with that . . . ?" but I had gone into the lavatory.

I sat down on the loo. Same old bat time, same old bat place. Good grief. In my despairosity I said out loud to myself, "What in the name of pantyhose is the point?" A voice from the next loo said, "Gee, is that you?"

It was Ellen. I grunted. But she was all chatty. Just because she has Dave the Laugh as a boyfriend. A dumpee of mine. She said through the wall, "Do you know what Dave says when he is leaving? Instead of saying good-bye?"

I wasn't remotely interested in what my castoffs said instead of good-bye. They are quite literally yesterday's news. Also, Ellen is in my bad books. I was giving her my cold shoulder. However, she was so interested in her new so-called boyfriend, Dave the so-called Laugh, that she hadn't noticed my shoulder. I thought if I flushed the loo she might get the hint, but she didn't.

"He says, 'Well, I'm off then. I'm away laughing on a fast camel.'" And she absolutely pissed herself laughing.

What is the matter with her? *Away laughing on a fast camel?*

assembly

9:00 a.m.

Fab news! Slim told us that some complete nutcase (Miss Wilson) is going to give us a special talk next week. About "reproduction."

Lord save us.

Slim also said Miss Wilson would be answering any questions we might have about "growing up and so on." Hahahahahahahaha. Hell could freeze over before I would ask Miss Wilson about my girlie parts.

After Slim had bored us to death for half an hour everyone else went off to English and I lolloped off slowly to her office for a spot of mental torture. I wasn't the only one waiting for a duffing; Jackie and Alison, the Bummer Twins, were sitting round in her anteroom. They looked at me when I sat down. Jackie said, "Oohhhh, what have you been up to, Big Nose?" She must die. She must die.

Then we heard the sound of a distant elephant (Slim), and Jackie stubbed out her fag and popped in a mint.

Slim said, "Come through, Georgia." Then she sat down at her desk and started writing. I just stood there. How many times had I been in this room for no good reason? Millions. Slim looked up and said, "Well," and I said, "Yes, milady?"

She glared at me. "What did you say?"

"Oh, sorry. I was just thinking about my English homework assignment, Miss Simpson."

She trembled in her jelloid way. It was amazing the way each chin could shake at a different rhythm. She said, "Well, it makes a change for you to think of anything serious or useful, Georgia."

Oh, that is so UNFAIR. What about all the hours I had spent thinking up the glove animal?

Slim was raving on, "I hope for a great improvement in your attitude to school and work after your suspension. I hope it has given you pause for thought. But first of all, you will go to Mr. Attwood and apologize to him for causing his injuries."

Oh great. Now I had to go and speak to the most bonkers man in the history of bonkerdom.

When I left her torture chamber Jackie Bummer said, "Did the nasty teacher tell you off and make you scared?" But when Slim shouted, "You two articles in here now!!!" they leapt up like two salmons.

Jas told me later that the Bummer Twins had arrived this morning, had a fag and then stuck a first-year to a bench with superglue.

9:35 a.m.

I walked really, really slowly along to Elvis's hut. At least if I took ages to find Elvis I might miss most of English. Sadly, that is when I saw his flat hat bobbling around. Not on its own, unfortunately; he was underneath it. Pushing his wheelbarrow along. I walked up quietly behind him and said really enthusiastically, "MR. ATTWOOD. HELLO!!!"

He leapt up like a perv in overalls (which he is). "What do YOU want?"

"Mr. Attwood, it's me!!!"

"I know who you are all right. Why are you shouting?"

"I thought you might have gone deaf."

"Well, I haven't."

"Well you might have. You see, I know what it's like at your stage of life—my grandad is deaf. And he's got bandy legs."

"Well, I'm not deaf. What do you want? I'm still not right, you know. My knee gives me awful gyp."

"Slim . . . er . . . Miss Simpson said I had to come and apologize."

"Yes, well, quite right, too." He was SO annoying. And a bit pingy pongoes when you got downwind of him.

I said, "So then. See you around."

He said, "Just a minute—you haven't said you are sorry yet."

"I have. I just told you I had to come and apologize."

"I know, but you haven't."

I said patiently, "Well, why am I here then? Am I a mirage?"

"No, you're not a mirage; you're a bloody nuisance."

"Thank you."

"Clear off. And you should behave a bit more like a young lady. In my day you would have—"

I interrupted him politely. "Mr. Attwood, interesting though the Stone Age is, I really haven't got time to discuss your childhood. I'll just say *au revoir* and if I don't see you again in this life, best of luck in that great caretakers' home in the sky."

He was muttering and adjusting his trousers (erlack!), but he shambled off. He daren't say too much to me because he suspects I have seen his nuddy mags, which I have.

lunchtime

Hours and hours of boredom followed by a cheese sandwich. That is what my morning has been like. And I wish Nauseating P. Green would stop ogling me. Blinking at me through her thick glasses like a goldfish in a uniform. Since I saved her from being duffed up by the Bummers last term she follows me round like a Nauseating P. Green on a string.

Rosie said to me, "She loves you."

Good Lord.

1:30 p.m.

Nauseating P. Green even followed me into the loos. As I was drying my hands she said, "Georgia, would you . . . would you . . . like to see some photos of my hamster? He's called Hammy."

Oh right, that's top of my list, photos of a hamster. I was going to say no, but she looked so blinky that I couldn't.

"P. Green."

"Yes?"

"Hammy has got about ten babies around him."

"I know; he's just had them."

Well, at least someone is going to be astonished by Miss Wilson's sex talk.

2:35 p.m.

Madame Slack was so overjoyed to see me that she made me sit right at the front next to Nauseating P. Green and Slack Alice, both of whom can only see the board if it's an inch away from their glasses. Jas and Ellen (Jas's bestest new lezzie mate) and the rest of the gang sat together at the back.

On the plus side, Madame Slack told us we are going to have a student teacher next week. That is usually *très amusant*. A bit of a light in a dark world.

4:00 p.m.

Bell rang.

At last escape from this hellhole. Jas and me were walking out of the gates when we saw Tom waiting for her. She went red as two short red things because she hadn't rolled her skirt over. She managed to pout though. Tom gave me a kiss on the cheek. *Mais oui!! Très* continental for someone who works part-time in a vegetable shop. He said, "Welcome back. You missed a cracking night at the cinema the other night. What did you get up to in Och Aye land?"

"I hung around a twenty-four-hour supermarket."

"Is that the groovy thing to do up there then?"

"No, it's the ONLY thing to do."

5:00 p.m.

Talk about being Queen of the Goosegogs. I had to walk along with Jas and Tom holding hands. (I don't mean we were all holding hands, although that would have been funnier.) I am giving Jas the cold shoulder as well as Ellen because of going to the cinema as a gang without the essential ingredient: me.

However, my shoulders are making little impression on anyone.

7:15 p.m.
Jas phoned.

"Gee."

"Yes, who is that?" (Even though I knew who it was.)

"It's me, Jas."

"Oh."

"Look, you could have come to the cinema with us, but you were in Och Aye land."

"Huh."

"And, well, it was just, you know, couples, and well, I don't think Robbie would have wanted to come. He doesn't really hang out with Tom much. You know Robbie's got his mates from The Stiff Dylans and because he's got the band and . . ."

She dribbled on for ages.

midnight
The nub and gist of Jas's pathetic apology is that I am going out with an older Sex God. We came to an understanding. The understanding is that she

has to show her remorse; she has to be my slavey girl for three days. And do everything I say.

tuesday november 2nd
lunchtime
I made slavey girl give me a piggyback to the loos. Hawkeye said we were "being ridiculous."

8:00 p.m.
The Sex God was waiting for me outside school!!! And he was in his cool car. Fortunately I had abstained from doing anything ridiculous with my beret. So I was able to get into his car only having to concentrate on not letting my nostrils flare too much . . . or knocking him out with my nunga-nungas. SHUT UP, BRAIN!!!

10:00 p.m.
I must stop being jelloid woman every time I see the Sex God. Why oh why did I say "I'm away laughing on a fast camel" instead of good-bye? What is the matter with me?

However, on the whole, taking things by and large . . . Yesssssssss!!!!!

I live at Snogging Headquarters. My address is:

> Georgia Nicolson
> Snogging Headquarters
> Snog Lane
> Snoggington

10:15 p.m.

Phoned Jas.

"Jas, I've done car snogging. Have you done that?"

"No. . . . I've done bike snogging."

"That's not the same."

"Oh. Why not?"

"It's just not the same."

"It is."

"No, it isn't."

"Well, there are still four wheels involved."

Good grief.

11:00 p.m.

In the car this afternoon Robbie put his head on my knee and sang me one of his songs. It was called "I'm Not There." I didn't tell Radio Jas that bit.

I never really know what to do with myself when he does his song singing. Maybe nod my head in time to the rhythm? How attractive is that from upside down? And also if you were passing the car as an innocent passerby you would just see my head bobbling round.

1:00 a.m.

Libby woke me up when she pattered and clanked into my room. When she had got everybody into my bed she said, in between little sobs, "Ohh, there was a big bad man, big uggy man."

She snuggled up really tightly and wrapped her legs round me. I gave her a big cuddle and said, "It's OK, Libbs, it was just a dream. Let's think about something nice. What shall we dream about?"

She said, "Porridge."

She can be so sweet. I gave her a little kiss on her cheek and she smiled at me (scary). Then she ripped the pillow from underneath my head so that Pantalitzer and scuba-diving Barbie could be comfy.

wednesday november 3rd

7:00 a.m.

Woke up with a crick in my neck and a sort of air-tank shape in my cheek where scuba-diving Barbie had been.

Dad came into the kitchen in a suit. Blimey. No one said anything. Apart from Libby, who growled at him. It turns out that it wasn't a nightmare she had last night. She just woke up and caught sight of Dad in his jimjams. Mum was in her usual morning dreamworld. As she came out of her bedroom getting ready for work, she was wearing her bra and skirt and nothing else. I said, "Mum, please, I'm trying to eat."

In the bathroom I checked the back of my head and profile. (There's a cabinet that has two mirrors on it. You can look through one and angle the other one so that you can look at the reflection of yourself sideways.) Then I put Mum's magnifying mirror underneath and looked down at myself, because say the Sex God had been lying on my knees sort of looking up at me adoringly and singing (which he had). Well, I wanted to know what that looked like.

I wish I hadn't bothered for two reasons: Firstly, when I looked down at the mirror I realized that my nose is GIGANTIC. It must have grown overnight. I look like Gerard Depardieu. Which is not a plus if you are not a forty-eight-year-old French bloke.

Secondly, you can definitely see my lurker from underneath.

8:18 a.m.

Jas was waiting for me at her gate. I was a bit aloof and full of maturiosity. Slavey girl said, "I've brought you a Jammy Dodger all to yourself."

"You can't treat me badly and then bribe me with a Jammy Dodger, Jas."

She can, though, because I was soon munching away.

On the way up the road I said to Jas, "Do you think my nose is larger than it was yesterday?"

She said, "Don't be silly. Noses don't grow."

"Well, everything else does—hair, legs, arms . . . nunga-nungas. Why should your nose be left out?"

She wasn't a bit interested. I went on, "And also can you see I have a lurker up my left nostril?"

She said, "No."

"But say you were sort of looking up my nose, from underneath."

She hadn't a clue what I was talking about. She has the imagination of a pea. Half a pea. We were just passing through the park and I tried to explain.

"Well, say I was singing. And you were the Sex God and you were lying with your head in my lap. Looking up adoringly. Marveling at my enormous talent. Waiting for the appropriate moment to leap on me and snog me to within an inch of my life."

She still didn't get it, so I dragged her over to a bench to illustrate my point. I made her put her head on my lap. I said, "So . . . what do you think?"

She looked up and said, "I can't hear you singing."

"That's because I'm not."

"But you said what if you were singing."

Oh for Goodness O'Reilly's trouser's sake!!! To placate her I sang a bit—the only thing that came into my head was "Goldfinger." It brought back horrible memories because Dad and Uncle Eddie had sung it the night Dad came home from Kiwi-a-gogo. They were both drunk and both wearing leather trousers, as Uncle Eddie said, "to impress the ladies." How sad and tragic is that?

Anyway, I was singing "Goldfinger" and Jas had her head on my lap looking up at my ever-expanding nostrils.

I said, "Can you see my lurker up there?"

Then we heard someone behind us having a fit. We leapt up. Well, I did. Jas crashed to the ground. It was Dave the Laugh, absolutely beside himself with laughing.

I said, "Er . . . I was just . . ."

Jas was going, "I was just looking up . . . Georgia's nose for . . . a . . . bit . . ."

Dave the L said, "Of course you were. Please don't explain. It will only spoil it for me." He walked along with us. I couldn't help remembering snogging him. And using him as a Red Herring. But he was funny. And he wasn't snidey. Just laughing a lot. In a Dave-the-Laugh way.

After he went off I said to Jas, "He seems to have forgiven me for being a callous minx, doesn't he? He is quite groovy-looking, isn't he?"

Uh-oh. I hope I am not becoming a nympho-whatsit. It is true though. I did think he looked quite cool. And a laugh. He's going to The Stiff Dylans gig this weekend. I said to Jas, "Do you think that he is going with Ellen?"

Why do I care? I am the girlfriend of a Sex God.

Still, I wonder if he is going with Ellen.

german

11:15 a.m.

To fill in the time whilst Herr Kamyer was writing something pointless on the blackboard about Helga and Helmut—Helga and Helmut are the HILARIOUS twins from our German language book called interestingly (NOT) *Helga and Helmut*. By the way, how many sausages can one person eat? Helmut is always stuffing one in his face. His lederhosen are probably as huge as Jas's pants. Anyway, as I say, to fill in the endless hours I gave Rosie a tattoo on her arm (in pen) of a lockjaw germ dancing. It was excellent. However, Jas (Mrs. Dense Knickers) said, "What is it?" My artistic talents are wasted on her. Also, and even more alarmingly, Jas seemed to be really interested in what happened to Helga and Helmut when they went shopping. I said to her, "They're not real, you know, Jas. They are German."

hockey

3:00 p.m.

Adolfa (Sports Oberführer and part-time lesbian) has been relatively quiet this term. She had extravagantly big shorts on today. As we got changed I said to Jas, "It's you she wants, Jas. I know because imitation is the sincerest form of flattery. Look at the size of her shorts. They are JUST like your knickers."

Jas hit me. Slavey girl is getting a bit uppity.

6:00 p.m.

Doing homework (peanut butter sandwich—making and hairstyling) with Ellen, Jas and Rosie. I casually found out that Ellen is meeting Dave the Laugh at the gig.

I said, "Oh, are you a sort of item then?"

She went a bit girlish. "Well, you know, he said, 'Are you going to the gig?' and I said, 'Yeah,' and he said, 'See you there then.'"

Rosie said, "Yes, but does he mean 'If you are going, I'll see you there because you will be like THERE to see'? Or does he mean 'See you there,' like in see YOU there?"

Ellen didn't know. She was in a state of confusosity. Join the club, I say.

As I wandered home I was thinking, one thing is true. He is not making the effort to meet her before the gig. Hahahahaha.

7:00 p.m.

Hang on a minute, though. Robbie has not arranged to meet me before the gig either. Is he expecting me to just turn up because I am, like, his official girlfriend? Oh well, it's only Wednesday. He'll call me and sort it out. Probably.

7:30 p.m.

Uh oh. Angus went on a kamikaze mission (kattikaze mission) to his beloved sex kitten. When he was let into the garden for his constitutional poo parlor division he burrowed under the fence. Pausing only to eat the Prat Poodles' supper and trap some voles, he went over to Mr. and Mrs. Across the Road's house. On to their roof.

He must have lurked up there until Mr. Across the Road came out to mow his lawn, and then dropped his love gifts (two voles and a half-eaten ham sandwich) onto Mr. Across the Road's head. Taking advantage of Mr. Across the Road's momentary blindness, he leapt into the house to be reunited with his beloved. Unfortunately, he was an unwelcome houseguest and in the ensuing struggle there was some incident with the cockatiel.

From what I can gather from Mr. Across the Road's shouting, it may never speak again. Which would be a plus in my book, as it only ever said, "Who's a pretty boy?"

10:00 p.m.
No call from Robbie.

I started softening up Dad for Saturday. "Vati, you know how hard I have been working at school . . . ? Well . . ."

He interrupted me. "Georgia, if this is leading up to any suggestion of quids leaping out of my pocket into your purse . . . forget it."

What an old miser.

"Vati, it's not to do with money. It's just that my friends and I are going to a gig on Saturday night and—"

"What time do you want me to pick you up?"

"It's alright, Dad. I'll just, you know, come home with the rest of the gang and . . ."

He's going to pick me up at midnight. It's hardly worth going out. I made him promise me that he'd crouch down behind the wheel and not get out of the car.

midnight

SG hasn't called me. How often should he call me? How often would I call him? About every five minutes seems right.

Maybe that's too keen. It implies I haven't got any sort of life.

12:05 a.m.

I haven't.

1:00 a.m.

OK, every quarter of an hour.

1:15 a.m.

It says in my *Men Are from Mars* book that boys don't need to talk as much as girls. The bloke that wrote it has obviously never met my uncle Eddie. When he came round the other day he didn't shut up for about five million years. He ruffles my hair. I am fourteen years old. Full of maturiosity. And snoggosity. I would ruffle HIS hair to show him how crap it is. But he hasn't got any.

thursday november 4th
operation glove animal

8:30 a.m.

This is GA Day (Glove Animal Day). Everyone is going to turn up with ears in place today. Jas was grumbling and groaning about getting a reprimand. I said, "Jas, please put your ears on as a smack in the gob often offends."

Even she got into the swing of it once her ears were in place. It was, it has to be said, quite funny. Jas looked hilarious bobbing along with her glove ears. She even did a bit of improvising with her teeth, making them stick out and doing nibbly movements with them like a squirrel. We did a detour through the back alleyway near the Science block. Elvis was in his hut reading his newspaper. We just stood there in our glove animal way looking in at him through the window. He sensed we were there and looked up. We stared back at him. His glasses were a bit steamed up, so maybe he really thought we were some woodland creatures. Woodland creatures who had decided to go to school and get ourselves out of our woodland poverty trap . . . But then he started shouting and raving on, "Clear off and learn something instead of messing about. And make yourselves look normal!!!"

Oh, wise advice from the looniest-looking person in the universe.

Unfortunately, Hawkeye spotted us before we could scuttle into the cloakroom. She went ballistic, unusually enough. I tried to explain that it was a useful way not to lose your gloves but I only got as far as "It's a really sensible way of . . ." before she snatched them off my ears. She has very little sense of humor.

However, the last laugh was on her because she was so busy telling me and Jas that we were ridiculously childish and ripping our ears off that she didn't see the rest of the ace gang bob into school. It was very, very funny indeed seeing them bob through the gates and across the playground as if they were perfectly normal glove animals.

7:00 p.m.
No call from the SG.

Mrs. Across the Road came over. Mutti had gone to her aerobics class. Surely it can't be healthy for a woman of her size to hurl herself around a crowded room.

Mrs. Across the Road or "Call me Helen" is OK but a bit on the nimby girlie side. If you hit her with a hockey stick she would probably fall over. She's fluffy and blond (not natural I think).

Vati was acting very peculiarly. He was being almost nice. And laughing a lot. And he got out of his chair. Hmmm. After she'd gone he must have said at least two hundred and fifty times, "She seems very nice, doesn't she? Helen? Very . . . you know . . . feminine."

Oh no.

Also he said that they are going to get a pedigree sort of boyfriend for Naomi. I said, "She won't go out with anyone else. She loves Angus."

Dad laughed. "You wait, there will be little Naomis running about the place before you can blink. Women are very fickle."

I said with great dignity, "Vati, different women have different needs."

He laughed in a most unpleasant way. "No, Georgia, all women have the same needs. They all need locking up."

Oh, *très, très* grown-up, Portly One.

9:10 p.m.

Pre-gig nervosity. Not helped by the fact that when I went down on to the field to take Angus for his prison recreation period, Mark Big Gob threw a Thunderball firework at me. It exploded right in front of me. Angus didn't even notice, but it nearly blew my lip gloss off. I wonder if Mark is quite normal in the brain department.

Oh God, I've just remembered it's Bonfire Night tomorrow, an excuse for all the sad boys in the world to set fire to themselves with fireworks whilst showing off to their mates.

9:30 p.m.

Mum came in flushed as a loon. I said, "You are looking particularly feminine, Mum." But Vati didn't get it.

in my room

9:50 p.m.

Vati knocked on my door!!! I said, "I'm sorry, but sadly I'm not in."

He ignored that (*quelle* surprise!) and came in and sat on the edge of my bed. Oh God, he wasn't going to ask me if I was happy, was he? Or tell me about his "feelings."

He was all embarrassed. "Look, Georgia, I know how you feel about Angus. . . ."

"Yes. And?"

"It's just not fair on him, being all cooped up in the house."

"Well, that is not my idea."

"I know, but he won't leave that bloody Burmese alone."

"He loves her and wants to share his life and dreams with her, maybe buy a little holiday home in Spain for those cold—"

"He's a bloody cat!!!"

10:00 p.m.

Dad is going to take Angus to the vet's tomorrow to have his trouser snake addendums taken away. He said, "I know you will think about this and be grown-up about it."

I said, "Dad, as I have mentioned before, if you do this to Angus you are no longer my vati. You are an ex-vati."

I mean it.

10:10 p.m.

Phone rang. Vati answered it, still all grumpy. I was in my room shaping the cuticles in my nails for Saturday. If I don't start my beauty routine now I'll never be ready in time. I heard Dad say, "I'll see if she's still up, it's a bit late to call. Who shall I say it is?"

By that time I had thrown myself down the stairs and ripped the phone out of his hand. How could he be so deeply uncool?

I calmed my voice and said hello, in a sort of husky way. I don't know why, but at least I wasn't assuming a French accent. It was the Sex God!!! Yeahhh!!! I got jelloid knickers as soon as I heard his voice. It's so yummy scrumboes. . . .

He said, "Is that your dad?"

I said, "No, it's just some madman who hangs around our house."

Anyway, the short and long of it is that he'll see me Saturday at the gig. He's rehearsing so can't see me before. *C'est la vie*, I think you will find, when you go out with *le* gorgeous popstar.

friday november 5th
bonfire night

4:00 p.m.

Some of the Foxwood lads sneaked into school today and put a banger down a loo and the loo exploded! You could hear the explosion even in the Science block. Slim was so furious that her chins practically waggled off.

6:30 p.m.

Vati has actually taken Angus to the vet. I cannot believe it. I am not speaking to him.

He said, "The vet said he would be fit as a flea on Monday, and we can pick him up then."

Libby and me might go on dirty protest, like they do in prison. Not bother going to the loo—as a protest, just poo on the floor. Mind you, Libby is almost permanently on dirty protest so they might not notice.

8:00 p.m.

Mutti and the bloke that she sadly lives with have gone to the street bonfire. Mr. and Mrs. Next Door and Mr. and Mrs. Across the Street and the saddos from number twenty-four are all going to be there and then they are off to a party at number twenty-six. Can you imagine the fun that will be? Vati was wearing a leather cowboy hat. How tragic is that? Very, very tragic. Mutti asked me if I was coming. I just looked at Dad's hat. Anyway, as I am not speaking to any of them I can't reply. Dad leapt over the garden wall instead of going through the gate. Sadly he didn't do himself a severe injury, and so he lives to embarrass me to death another day.

Angus normally loves Bonfire Night.

Does he know his bottom-sniffing days are over?

8:30 p.m.

Jools, Rosie and Jas came round. They're all off to a bonfire party at Kate Matthews's place. SG is rehearsing again, but we're going to meet up later. The girls managed to find something to eat in the kitchen, which is a bloody miracle.

We sat munching and crunching our cornflake sarnies. Jools said, "I must get a boyfriend. I quite fancy that mate of Dave the Laugh's. What is he called . . . is it Rollo? You know, the one that's got a nice smile."

He was quite cool-looking, now she mentioned it. I said, "I wonder why he hasn't got a girlfriend. Maybe there is something wrong with him."

Jools was all alert. "Like what?"

"Well, you know Spotty Norman who has acne of the head?"

"Rollo hasn't got any spots."

"He might have secret acne."

"Secret acne?"

"Yeah, it only starts at the top of his arms."

"Who gets acne like that?"

"Loads of people."

"Like who?"

"Loads of people."

Actually I noticed that Rosie had a bit of a lurker on her chin. She had been poking it about and I told her she shouldn't do that. She should try my special lurker eradicator. You squirt perfume on the lurker. Really loads and loads and that dries it up. In theory. I used it on my nostril lurker and it worked a treat. Mind you, in the process I practically choked to death on Paloma (Mum's).

my bedroom

10:00 p.m.

The sky is lit up with rockets from people's firework parties. And I am alone in my room. I'm very nearly a hermitess. SG's rehearsal has run on, so we can't meet up. Still, I'm not going to mope round. I'm going to do something creative with poster paints.

11:30 p.m.

When Mutti and Vati came in I didn't speak to them. I just unfurled the CAT MOLESTERS banner I had made.

saturday november 6th

11:00 a.m.

The cat molesters went off shopping.

1:00 p.m.

I'd better start my makeup soon. It's only seven hours till the gig. But as I fully expect to be snogged to within an inch of my life, what about snogproof makeup? As Billy Shakespeare said, "To lippy or not to lippy; that is the question."

Rang Jas. Her mum called her and she eventually shambled to the phone. I said, "Oh, glad you could make it, Jas. My eyebrows have grown to the floor in the time it took you to get here."

Jas, as usual, took offense. "I was in my bedroom just working something out on the computer with Tom."

I laughed sarcastically. "Jas, you only snog in your bedroom."

"We don't."

"You do. Anyway, lots of fun though this is, I want to ask you something of vital importance to the universe. Well, my universe, anyway. What do you think about lippy and snogging?"

"What?"

"Well, do you put lippy on and then do you wipe it off before lip contact, or do you let it go all over Tom's face and Devil take the hindmost?"

2:00 p.m.
Results of lippy/snogging poll:

Jas only wears lip gloss, which she says gets absorbed in the general snogosity. Rosie says she puts on lippy AND lip gloss, then just goes for full-frontal snogging with Sven. She also says that by the end of the night he is usually covered in lippy, but he doesn't mind and wipes it off with his T-shirt.

Good Lord.

We must remember, however, that he is not English.

The rest of the gang seemed pretty well to go along with the lip gloss absorbed into the general snogosity theory.

So lip gloss it is.

3:00 p.m.
Surrounded by hair products.

My hair will not go right. It has no bounce-ability. It just lies there. Annoying me with its lack of bounceability.

Sacré bloody *bleu*. I won't be able to go out unless it starts bouncing about a bit. I look like a Franciscan monk. Or Miss Wilson.

I'm going to stick some of Mum's hot rollers in it.

4:30 p.m.
On my bed in rollers. V. attractive.

Reading my book *Don't Sweat the Small Stuff for Teens* to cheer me up. And calm me down.

4:45 p.m.

Hey, there is a chapter about hair! Honestly! How freaky deaky is that?

It's called "Be OK with Your Bad Hair Day."

5:00 p.m.

The short and short of it is that we are obsessed with our looks and imagine that other people really care about what our hair looks like.

But they don't!!

So that is OK then. Took out my rollers.

5:10 p.m.

Vati bounced into my room (not knocking, of course) and said, "Tea is on the—what in the name of arse have you done to your head? You look like you have been electrocuted."

I hate my dad. Twice.

5:30 p.m.

Time for my pore-tightening mask. (Because there is nothing worse than loose pores.)

I lay there with my pores tightening. In the book it recommends yoga for inner harmony. I must start doing it again.

5:35 p.m.

Mind you, the author says he is "super glad" that he took up yoga at a young age.

5:37 p.m.

Perhaps he is a "super tosser."

5:39 p.m.

Or am I being "supercritical?"

Who knows.

Phoned Jools with my pore-tightening mask still on, trying not to crack it. Dad was pretending to be an orangutan (not much pretending needed) as a "laugh." I ignored him. I said to Jools, "Nyut nar nu naring?"

"Purple V-necked top. Purple hipsters."

Hmm.

Phoned Rosie, "Nut nar nu noing nid nor nair?"

"Pigtails."

Crikey. We seem to be running the gamut of style from hippie to Little Bo Peep and beyond.

6:00 p.m.

I've tried on every single thing in my wardrobe. Oh buggery, I am in a state of confusosity. I wish I had a style counselor. I'm going to get one when I appear at record awards ceremonies with the Sex God. It won't be Elton John's style counselor. It will be someone normal. And stylish. And a good counselor.

6:30 p.m.

I've decided to go for the radically sophisticated look for the gig (i.e., all black). With, for special effect, black accessories (providing I can sneak out with Mum's Chanel bag without her noticing).

6:35 p.m.

I'm wearing a V-necked black leather vest, short skirt and boots. What does that say about me? Casual sophisticate? Inner vixen struggling to get out? Girlfriend of a Sex God?

Or twit?

6:38 p.m.

I wonder what SG will be wearing. What does it matter? We are all in the nuddy-pants under our clothes.

I LOVE his mouth. It's so yummy and sort of curly and sexy. And it's mine, all mine!!! Mind you, I love his hair, so black and gorgey. And his eyes . . . that deep deep blue . . . mmmmm . . . dreamsville. And his eyelashes. And his arms. And his tongue . . . In fact, there isn't one bit of him I don't like. Of all the bits I've seen, anyway.

I wonder what his favorite bit of me is? I should emphasize it.

My eyes are quite nice. My nose, yes, well, we'll just skip over that. Mouth . . . mmm, a bit on the generous side, but that can be a good thing.

6:45 p.m.
Phoned Jas. "Jas, what do you think is my best feature? Lips? Smile? Casual sophisticosity?"

"Well, I don't know what to say now, because I was going to say your cheeks."

Good grief.

6:50 p.m.
Phoned Jas again.

"What do you think on the basooma front? You know, emphasize them, do the 'Yes, I've got big nunga-nungas, but I'm proud of them!' or strap them down and don't breathe out much all night?"

That's when Vati went ballisticisimus about me

being on the phone. "Why the hell do you talk rub-bish to Jas on the phone when she is coming round here in a minute and you can talk rubbish to her without it costing me a fortune?!!!!"

It's not me that talks rubbish. It's him. He just shouts rubbish at me. He's like Hawkeye with a beard.

I said to Mutti, "Why doesn't the man you live with go for a job as a combination cat molester and teacher?"

beautosity headquarters
7:00 p.m.

Jas came round to my house for us to walk to the clock tower together. Also I needed her for a cosmetic emergency. I had forgotten to paint my toenails, and my skirt was so tight I couldn't bend my leg up far enough to get to my toes. I suppose I could have taken my skirt off, but what are friends for?

I am too giddy and girlish with excitement to paint straight anyway. We went into the front room, which is warmer than my room. Mind you so is Siberia.

Vati was watching the news. Huh. Jas started

on toenail duty. I thought a subtle metallic purple would be nice. Robbie would think that was cool if my tights fell off for some reason. Anyway, then it said on the news, "And tonight the Prime Minister has just got to Number Ten."

I looked down at Jas and said, "Ooer." Meaning he'd got to number ten on the snogging scale. And then we both laughed like loons.

Vati just looked at us like we were mad.

clock tower

8:00 p.m.

Met the rest of the ace gang and we ambled off to the gig. This was my first official outing as girlfriend of a Sex God. I wasn't going to let it go to my head though.

Lalalalalalalala. Fabbity fab fab. Eat dirt, Earth creatures.

When we got to the Buddha Lounge the first "person" I saw was . . . Wet Lindsay. Robbie's ex. There is always a wet fish in every ointment. Every cloud has got a slimy lining. She has got the tiniest forehead known to humanity. She is quite literally fringe and then eyebrow. She was talking to her equally sad mates Dismal Sandra and Tragic Kate.

Every time I look at Wet Lindsay I am reminded that underneath her T-shirt lurk breast enhancers.

I said to Jas, "Do you think that Robbie knows about her false nunga-nungas?" but she was too busy waving at Tom with a soppy smile on her face.

The club was packed. I wondered if I should go find Robbie and say hello. Maybe that wasn't very cool. Better do a bit of makeup adjusting first. Because if the talent scout was there he might be looking for girls to form a band as well. I said that to Jas. "Maybe we could be discovered, as a new girl band."

"We can't sing or play any instruments, and we are not in a band."

She is so ludicrously picky.

It was mayhem in the loos. You couldn't get near the mirrors for love or money. The Bummers were in there, of course, larding on the foundation. Alison must use at least four pounds of it trying to conceal her huge lurkers. Or am I being a bit harsh?

No . . . I am being accurate. And factual.

I came out of the loos into the club. It was very dark; you needed to be half bat to find your way round. And then, shining like a shining Sex God in trousers, I saw him. Tuning his guitar. He looked up and saw me and smiled. I went over and he grabbed me and dragged me into a room. ("Oh stop it, stop it!" I yelled . . . not.) It was The Stiff Dylans' dressing room. I'd never been backstage before. I suppose I will have to get used to it.

We did some excellent snogging (six and a half) but then he had to go and tune up with the rest of the band. He said, "See you on my break."

When I went back to the loos my lip gloss had completely gone!!! Absorbed in the snoggosity.

9:00 p.m.

Yeah! What a dance fest! I was so shattered after being thrown around by Sven that I had to go and have a little sit down in an alcove with Rosie and Jas.

I could see Wet Lindsay and her wet mates dancing right in front of the stage. How desperate was that? In fact, it was all girls at the front, most of them dancing around in front of my Sex God. Smiling up at him and shaking their bums round. But he only had eyes for me. Well, he would have done, had he had a talking sniffer dog that could have come round and found me sitting in the dark behind a pillar, and gone back and told SG where I was. There was an older bloke in a suit standing by the side of the stage. I bet he was the talent scout.

I said to Jas, "Come and dance in front of the talent scout with me."

She said, "No."

"Jas."

"No, and what is more . . ."

"What?"

"No."

"It's no then, is it, Mrs. Huge Knickers? Well, when I am happily being a backup dancer I will think of you packing potatoes."

She ignored me, but as I say, *In vino veritas.* I don't know why because I am really crap at Latin (according to Slim, spokeswoman for the Latin people).

Well, as usual, I would have to step boldly where no woman had stepped before. I went over and gave my all in front of the talent scout in a triumph of dance casualosity. He seemed quite impressed, but then he went off to the dressing rooms. Probably phoning his record company.

Phew, it was hot and sweaty. I nipped off to the

loos to make sure my glaciosity was still in place and I didn't look like a red-faced loon. My waterproof eyeliner seemed to be holding its own. Rosie was readjusting her piggies next to me in the mirror so I asked her, "Does Sven ever make you jealous?"

"No, not really. He's sort of quite grown-up in his own way."

As we came out of the loos we could see Sven almost immediately. He was in the middle of a big group balancing a drink on his head and doing Russian dancing. It's a mystery to me how he manages to get down so low, his jeans are so tight.

The Bummers were talking to some really lardy-looking blokes in leather jackets. They all had fags. You could hardly see their heads for smoke. Which was a plus. I did make out that one of the lardheads had a mustache. I shouted to Jools, "Imagine snogging someone with a mustache."

And she said, "What, like Miss Stamp?"

9:30 p.m.

Jools had been looking at Rollo for about a million centuries and moaning and droning on about him. He was hanging out with a bunch of lads round the bar. I was trying to concentrate on looking at the Sex God. He is sooooo cool. He's by far the coolest in the band. Dom, Chris and Ben are all quite groovy-looking but they don't have that certain *je ne sais quoi* that the Sex God has. That extra snogosity. That puckery gorgeosity combined with fabulosity. That sexgoderosity.

Jools didn't seem to know I was in Snog Heaven because she was rambling on. "He's quite fit, isn't he?"

"Yeah, he's gorgeous and he's all mine, mine, miney."

"Gee, I mean Rollo, you banana."

I was less than interested but she went on and on. "Should I go across?"

Pause.

"Or is that too pushy?"

Pause.

"I think it's always best to play a bit hard to get, don't you? Yes, that's how I'll play it. He'll have to beg to get my attention."

9:35 p.m.
Jools was sitting on Rollo's knee and snogging for England. Oh well. As I said to Ellen, "She's

obviously gone for the playing-hard-to-get-ticket."

9:39 p.m.

Tom told me that the "talent scout" was Dom's dad who helps with the band's equipment. He told Dom he thought I was trying to get off with him. OhmyGodohmyGod. I would now have to spend the rest of the night and probably the rest of my life not looking at Dom's dad.

I told Ellen, but she was too busy waiting for Dave the Laugh to show up. I must have been to the loos with her about a hundred times just in case she has missed him in the dark somewhere.

I am without doubt a great mate. You wouldn't get Jas trailing backwards and forwards to the loos. Mostly because she seems to be glued to Tom. She has very little pride.

Quite a few lads have asked me to dance. Well, their idea of asking me to dance, which means they hang round showing off when I'm dancing with my mates. I must have that thing that you can get. You know, like baboons. When female baboons are in the mood they get a big red bottom and then the male baboons know they are in the mood and gather round. Yes, that must be it—I must have the metaphorical red bottom because of the Sex God.

10:00 p.m.

On his break Robbie came offstage and he looked over at me. This was it, this was the moment that everyone would know I was his girlfriend!! At last all my dreams were beginning to come true. I was going to be the official girlfriend (OG)!! No more hiding our love from the world. Just snogging-a-gogo and Devil take the hindmost. I couldn't wait to see Wet Lindsay's face when Robbie came over to me. Tee hee. Yessss!!!!

In the meantime I lived in Cool City. I was sipping my drink and pretending to talk to Jas and Tom, although every time Jas said anything it really annoyed me. I'd say, "OhmyGodohmyGod, I think he's coming over. . . . Oh, that absolutely useless tart Sammy Mason is thrusting herself at him now."

And Jas would say, "She's actually quite a nice person, really good at blodge."

Ludicrous, stupid, pointless things she was saying. In the end I said, "Jas, can you just pretend to talk to me, but don't say anything in case I have to hit you."

Now there was a whole group of girls round Robbie, giggling and jiggling about in front of him! Then Wet Lindsay slimed up. And actually touched his cheek. My boyfriend's cheek she touched. With her slimy hand. Tom said, "Leave it, Gee, just be cool. Honestly, he'll like it better if you don't make a fuss."

Huh. What did Hunky know about it? Then he said, "Besides which, you're not long off your stick, and she will definitely kill you."

Fair point. She had deliberately and viciously whacked me round the ankles in a hockey match last month and I didn't want to be hobbling round for another two weeks.

I couldn't bear the tension of waiting for Robbie to come over; it made me really need to go to the piddly diddly department. I nipped off to the loos. A minute or two later Rosie came in, and she wasn't alone; she had Sven with her. He said, "Oh *ja*, here ve is in the girlie piddly diddlys."

He scared four girls, who went screeching out.

He is a very odd Norwegian-type person. Perhaps they have whatsits in Norwayland? You know, bisexual lavatories. Do I mean that or unicycle lavatories? No . . . unisex lavs, I mean. Rosie was completely unfazed by him being there, but as we all know she is not entirely normal herself. She said, "Robbie says he will see you in the dressing room."

Oh hell's biscuits. Pucker alert, pucker alert!! After an emergency reapplication of lip gloss I made my way to the dressing room. I just got near when I saw Lindsay was there again! This time fiddling around with his shirt collar.

Unbelievable.

Robbie caught my eye and raised his eyebrows to me and then behind her back gave me like a "wait five minutes" sign with his hand.

10:02 p.m.
I was livid as an earwig on livid pills.

Wait five minutes because of her . . . ?

Unbelievable.

10:05 p.m.
Back on the dance floor all my so-called mates were too busy snogging their boyfriends to listen to me complain. OK, I would have to take action on

my own. I said to Jas over Tom's shoulder because they were slow dancing, "I will not, definitely not, play second fiddle to a stick insect."

She said, "What are you going to do then?"

I had to sort of dance along with them in order to keep up with where her head was. "I'm going to be absent. Upstairs. Don't tell him where I am if he asks you." Then I hid upstairs in the club. I got a few funny looks from the snoggers up there as I crouched down by the stairs, but I didn't care.

I could look down and see Robbie looking for me. He even sent Jas into the loos to see if I was in there. She did a ludicrous comedy wink up at me as she went. What is she thinking? If she had been a spy in the war, German high command would have only had to get on the blower to her and say, "Vat haf you been told never to divulge?" and she would tell them everything, probably including the Queen's bra size (sixty-four double-D cup).

Anyway, I could see Robbie getting more and more worked up about not finding me. Ha and triple ha. Hahahahaha, in fact. So, Mr. Sex God, the worm is for once on the other foot.

On the downside I had managed to make myself a snog-free zone.

10:20 p.m.

After the SG had gone back onstage to play another set, I went into the loos. Ellen was in there looking all mournful. She said, "I'm going to go. Dave the L hasn't turned up. He said he would see me here, and he hasn't come."

I tried wisdomosity about elastic bands and when a boy says "see you" who knows what that means, etc., etc. but she wasn't interested.

She went off home all miserable.

Honestly, you try to help people even though you have troubles enough of your own. (And even though some people bring things on themselves because they get off with their best mate's red herrings.)

When I came out of the loos I made sure that Robbie could see how miffed I was. He tried his heartbreaking smile on me, but I ignored him with a firm hand and pretended to be laughing with my mates. I said to Rosie, "Wet Lindsay is a crap dancer, and her hair has no bounceability. Neither incidentally, despite all her efforts, have her basoomas. They just lie there. I think a bit of bounce in a basooma is a good thing."

I wondered what level of bounceability mine

had when I was dancing. I went to a dark corner at the back of the bar where no one was to inspect them whilst I danced. Well, they certainly did jiggle, not always in time to the music either. Perhaps if I kept my shoulders rigid they would keep still. As I was trying rigid shoulder dancing Dave the Laugh turned up. I was so shocked I went, "Where have you been?"

He grinned. He looked very cool in black. He said, "Why? Did you miss me? Mrs. Dumper." But he didn't seem bitter or anything. Perhaps he had forgiven me. He said, "God, it's hot in here. Do you fancy a cold drink?"

Well, no harm in a cold drink with an old dumpee is there?

Jas ogled me as I went off to the bar with him, but I just ogled back. Honestly, she acts like she's fifty. She'll start wearing head scarves soon and discussing the price of potatoes with anyone who will listen (i.e., no one). Anyway, if the Sex God could hang out with his exes, so could I.

Dave the L and I took our drinks outside for a breath of fresh air. I sort of said awkwardly, "Dave, I'm really sorry for, you know, using you like a Red Herring."

He said, "Yes, well . . . I was pretty upset at the time."

He seemed unnaturally serious. Oh God's pajamas. I was meant to be having a laugh. Why was he called Dave the Laugh if he was not a laugh? He should have been called Dave the Unlaugh. Shut up, brain.

I said, "Well, you know I just—"

He interrupted me, "Georgia, there is something you should know—I . . ."

Oh God. OhGoddyGodGod. He sounded like he was going to cry. What should I do? I hadn't been to boy-crying classes; I only went to snogging ones. I looked down at my drink and I could sort of sense him putting his head in his hands. I was just staring at my drink and avoiding looking at him. Then he said in a low sort of broken voice, "I haven't been able to get over you. . . . I think—I think . . . I'm in love with you."

Oh *sacré* bloody *bleu* and triple *merde*. I mumbled, "Dave, I don't know what to say. I, well . . . I . . ."

He said, "Perhaps if you could give me just one last kiss."

I looked round at him. And he looked at me.

And he was wearing a big red false clown's nose.

Actually it was really, really funny, even though the joke was on me. He just looked hilarious!! Both of us were falling about.

But then this awful thing happened. I accidentally found myself attached to his mouth. (He took the red nose off first though.)

midnight

I was in such a tizz of a spaz that I was on time outside for when Vati turned up. Is it really necessary for him to wear a balaclava? And also it's like being on a quiz show; he kept asking me things. "So did you have fun then? Did any lads ask you to dance?"

Why does he want to know everything? I'm not interested in him; why is he so interested in me? I would tell him what a complete fiasco he is making of himself, but I'm not speaking to him so I can't.

Anyway, if he did know that I had been snogging he would probably tie me to the kitchen table like Angus. Or take me to the vet's.

1:00 a.m.

I didn't say good night or anything to Robbie. I just couldn't. I didn't say anything to Dave the Laugh either. After the accidental snog I was in a sort of a daze. Dave the Laugh seemed a bit surprised, too. He said, "Er . . . right . . . well . . . I think I'll just, like . . . er . . . at . . . go to the . . ."

And I said, "Yes, er. I think . . . I'll like, you know . . . just er . . . you know, go and . . . er . . . go . . ."

But neither of us knew what we were talking about.

This time my big red bottom has taken things too far.

2:00 a.m.

Am I a scarlet-bottomed vixen?

What will I say to Robbie?

2:30 a.m.

For heaven's sake. It was just a little kiss! I am a teenager, I've got whatsit . . . lust for life. Also it was probably my hormones that made me do it (Officer).

3:00 a.m.

What's a little kiss between exes?

3:01 a.m.

And a tiny bit of tongues.

3:03 a.m.

And nip libbling.

3:05 a.m.

NIP LIBBLING??? What in the name of Jas's commodious panties am I talking about? You see. I am so upset I have got internal dyslexia. I mean lip nibbling, not nip libbling.

Anyway, I am not alone on the Guilt Train because Dave the Laugh is also on it. He is a two-timer with Ellen.

3:10 a.m.

Oh God, she is my mate. I am bad bad baddy bad bad. Jesus would never snog his mate's boyfriend.

3:15 a.m.

I will probably never be able to sleep again.

Zzzzzzzzzzzzzz.

sunday november 7th

9:00 a.m.

The phone rang. Libby answered it. "Heggo? Yes yes yes yes yes yes yes yes, listen."

I could hear her singing her version of "Dancing Queen," and there was a sort of banging noise as well—she would be doing the accompanying dance. God help the poor sod who was on the other end of the phone.

"Dancing bean . . . dancing bean . . . feel the touch of my tangerine . . . ine . . ."

It was so loud that even Mutti was forced to get up to try to shut her up. She said, "Libby, let Mummy talk." There was the sound of a struggle and spitting and then I heard Mum say, "Hello? Oh yes, well hang on. I'll see if she's up." She shouted up the stairs, "Georgia, it's Robbie for you."

I shot out of bed and downstairs. Checking in the mirror to make sure I didn't have idiot hair. Although that meant the Sex God would have X-ray vision if he could see down the telephone. Perhaps he did have extrasensory whatsit and he would sense my red-bottomosity. Oh God. The Sex God!!! As she handed over the phone Mum winked at me. Shutupshutup winking.

I tried not to sound like a scarlet minx. I wanted to achieve casualosity with a hint of maturiosity. With no suggestion of red-bottomosity.

"Hi." (How cool is that? V. cool, that's how.)

"Georgia? What happened last night? Where were you? Jas said that you got in trouble with your dad and had to leave."

Phew. For once in her life Jas had actually done something right.

I said, "Er . . . yes, he got the mega hump like he always does and, er . . . well, actually if I hadn't have gone he would have come in and danced and no one wants to see him doing the Twist." What in the name of Beelzebub was I talking about?

Robbie seemed to relax then. He said, "Listen, I'm really sorry about last night. I really wanted to be round you and then there was the Lindsay thing . . . and the bloke from the record company being there. He wanted to speak to us after the gig."

Anyway, it was really dreamy talking to him. The record bloke wants to sign up The Stiff Dylans.

Wow!!

Robbie said he would meet me at the bottom of the hill at lunchtime.

10:30 a.m.
Mutti followed me into my bedroom. She said, "So, Robbie . . . hmmm. Who is he then? Which school does he go to? He sounds quite sexy on the phone." (Erlack, my parents are OBSESSED with sex.) I went on applying my natural-looking makeup (just a hint of daytime glitter). I am not officially speaking to her either (as she is the cat molester's handmaiden). Except to ask her for my pocket money.

Mum went raving on. "Look, come on, love, stop sulking. It was the only thing to do. It's cruel to keep a wild animal cooped up all the time."

I said, "Well, let Vati go and have a sniff round in the garden then."

She went all parenty. "It's not funny to be so rude. We are only trying to do our best." She looked like she was going to cry as she went out.

Oh poo. Poo and *merde*.

10:00 p.m.
It was fab!!! Being with my BOYFRIEND. And what is fabbier is that we bumped into a couple of

Robbie's mates and went round to their house. Dom was there from The Stiff Dylans. He looked at me a bit funny. I wonder if he thinks I really want to get off with his dad. Oh *sacré bleu*. No one else was there that I knew; they were mostly much older than me. How cool is that? And Robbie was holding my hand!!! In front of them!!!

One of them asked me what I was going to do at university. Er. I said, "Backup dancing." I don't know why.

I didn't say anything else after that. I just smiled like an imbecile a lot.

Dom and Robbie talked about their record deal. They're all really nice. Then John asked me if I smoked and I said only if my hair is on fire, and they just looked at me.

11:30 p.m.
SG said he really rates me. He did the neck-kissing stuff and ear snogging. It was so dreamy. My only slight worry is Rosie's theory of things growing if they get snogged (like your lips). If he goes on snogging my ears, will I get elephant ears?

midnight

Lalalalalalalalalalala.

12:30 a.m.

I closed my eyes and started doing dreamy dreamy about snogging the SG. Doing a sort of rerun of the highlights. Mmmm. But then as Robbie stuck his tongue in one ear Dave the Laugh appeared out of nowhere. And stuck his tongue in my other ear.

12:45 a.m.

Like an ear kabob.

1:15 a.m.

That is it. I have put my red bottom to bed. It will not be rearing its ugly head again.

My nip libbling days are over.

I am and always will be the girlfriend of a Sex God.

The End.

1:30 a.m.

Still, it's a bit weird being with people older than me.

monday november 8th

7:45 a.m.

Woken at the crack of dawn by Vati yelling and carrying on downstairs. He was singing, "The boys are back in town, the boys are back in town. Yesssssss! Owzat!!!!!!!! The boy's a genius!!!!!!"

It turns out some fool has offered him a job. He is going to be in charge of waterworks or something. I said, "We'd better dig a well then."

But M and V were too busy snogging each other to hear me. Erlack a pongoes. Also they seem to be failing to notice that they do not exist for me.

Vati was UNBEARABLE at breakfast, wearing his dressing gown slung round his shoulders like a sort of prizefighter and lifting Libby above his head with one hand. Actually, that bit was quite funny because she clung on to the overhead lamp and wouldn't let go, and he very nearly lost his rag. I think he must be in some sort of hormonal middle-age thing because his moods are very unpredictable. One minute it's all jokes; the next minute you ask him for a measly fiver and he goes ballistic. He is alarmingly bonkers. And chubby. And a cat molester.

8:15 a.m.

Met Jas. She said, "I told Robbie what you told me to, but I still don't understand why you had to rush off."

"Dad had got his balaclava on."

"Oh right, I see. Yes."

And alarmingly she seemed quite satisfied. That is the trouble with telling people porkies—it is so easy. Should I confess about Dave the Laugh? Jas is my best friend. We know everything about each other. I, for instance, have seen her knickers. But on the other hand, she can be a terrible pain about morals and stuff. She might say it wasn't very nice of me as Ellen is my friend, etc., etc.

Hmmm. I'll think about it later. In the next life.

assembly

9:00 a.m.

Ellen said, "Sorry I was a bit moody and stressy with you on Saturday; I know you were just trying to cheer me up. Dave the Laugh turned up just after I'd gone. Typical!"

OhmyGod. I am a facsimile of a sham of a friend.

french

1:30 p.m.

The whole school has gone bonkers!!! Our new student French teacher turns out to be a David Ginola look-alike!!! Honestly. He's bloody gorgeous. When he walked in even Rosie stopped plucking her eyebrows. Monsieur "Pliss Call Me Henri" has got sort of longish hair and really tight blue jeans. We are keen as *la moutarde* on French now. Any time he asks anything everyone puts their hands up. I can't remember the last time I saw anyone put their hand up in French. Usually we put our heads on our desks for a little snooze and just let our arms flop over if we are supposed to be answering anything. It's our little way of letting Madame Slack know how interested we are in Patapouf and Clicquot. Or whatever sad French people she is talking about.

break

2:30 p.m.

And it isn't just us—you should see the teachers. I even saw Hawkeye giggling when she was talking to Pliss Call Me Henri!

The saddest of all is Herr Kamyer, who has

gone completely giddy at having another man in the building. Unfortunately, his idea of bonding involves a lot of spasmodic dithering about and saying "Oh, *ja*. Oh, *ja sehr* interestink, Henri."

When Monsieur Henri opened the staff room door for Miss Wilson, her tragic seventies bob nearly fell off. They are all being pathetic, pretending to be interested in garlic and Edith Piaf and so on. Sad.

I, of course, as anyone who knows me will tell you, have always loved *la belle* France.

4:40 p.m.

On the way home I said to Jas, "I have always *aim*ed *la belle* France."

"You said you didn't like it because it was full of French people."

"Well, there is that, but apart from that I *aime* it very much."

dinnertime

6:00 p.m.

I said to Mutti, "Can we have wine with our fish fingers like they do in *la belle* France?"

She just said, "Don't be ridiculous."

6:20 p.m.

Vati is bringing Angus home from the vet's tonight. Libby and me have made a hospital bed sort of thing out of his cat basket and some old blankets. Libby put one-eyed Teddy in it as well.

He'll be so sad and probably in agony. He will be a facsimile of a sham of his former cathood. He will just be like other cats now. Not the magnificent half cat–half Labrador that he used to be.

I said to Mutti, "I hope it will not put you off your beauty regime, having Angus's trouser snake addendums on your conscience."

7:30 p.m.

Hahahahahaha. Angus leapt out of his cat cage and immediately attacked Vati's trousers. When Dad went to put the car in the garage Angus shot out into the garden and over the wall. I heard Snowy and Whitey yapping and Mr. Next Door yelling.

Happy days!

my bedroom
7:50 p.m.

Although it's a laugh having the French heart-throb around, it hasn't quite taken my mind off my unfaithfulness with Dave the L. I don't know what to do. Am I the only person who has a secret red bottom? Oh, I have such guiltosity.

8:00 p.m.

How can I concentrate on my French homework? Even if I had remembered to bring it home from school with me.

In my book about not sweating the small stuff it says, "Don't keep your pain a secret."

Rang Jas. Even she is quite swoony about Henri. "He's quite, you know . . . handsome, isn't he? In a French way."

I said, "*Mais oui. Très sportif.* Er . . . but lots of *les garçons* are, aren't they? It's natural at our age to be attracted to good-looking guys."

Jas was raving on, unaware of my secret pain. "No, I don't think so. It's only Tom for me. He is my one and only Hunky."

Good Lord. I said. "Yes, but you said Henri was quite handsome."

"I know, but that is just fantasy, isn't it? I wouldn't dream of doing anything about it."

"Yes, but what if, for instance, it was hot and you thought he was going to say he loved you and then you noticed he was wearing a red false nose. What then?"

She pretended not to know what I was talking about. I must bear my secret burden of pain alone. *Quel dommage.*

One thing is for sure, I must never speak to Dave the Laugh again. I must eschew him with a firm hand.

9:00 p.m.

Dave the Laugh rang!

Uh-oh. He said, "Georgia. I just rang to say don't worry about anything. I know how weird you can get. But it's OK. We just had a laugh. No one needs to know anything about it. We can be mates. Don't worry, Mrs. Mad."

Crikey. How grown-up is that? Scarily grown-up.

He's right though. I am just too sensitive for my own good. I should relax. It was just a little kiss.

9:05 p.m.

And lip nibble. With a hint of tongues.

But that is all.

11:05 p.m.

I wonder what number on the snogging scale nip libbling should be.

11:10 p.m.

Emergency snogging scale update:

(1)   holding hands

(2)   arm around

(3)   good-night kiss

(4)   kiss lasting over three minutes without a breath

(5)   open-mouth kissing

(6)   tongues

(6¼) nip libbling

(6½) ear snogging

(7)   upper body fondling—outdoors

(8)   upper body fondling—indoors (in bed)

(9)   below waist activity (b.w.a.) and

(10) the full monty

midnight

I wonder if it is possible to have two boyfriends. I mean, times are changing. Relationships are more complicated. In France men always have mistresses and wives and so on. Henri probably has two girlfriends. He would laugh if you told him you just had the one. He would say, *"C'est très, très tragique."*

So if he can have two I could have two. What is good for *le* gander must be *bon* for *la* goose *aussi. Je pense.* Oh, *merde.*

But would I want Robbie to have another girl-friend? No!!!!!

tuesday november 9th
7:50 a.m.
Angus is amusing himself by ambushing the post-man. Och aye, they may have taken his trouser snake addendums, but they cannae tak his freedom!!

walking to school with jas
8:30 a.m.
Jas was having a bit of fringe trouble (i.e., she had cut it herself and made herself look like Richard II), so she was even more vague than normal. She just went fringe fiddle, fringe fiddle. I was going to have to kill her. In a caring way. Oh, the burden of guilt. I wanted to shout out, "OK!! I have nip libbled with Dave the Laugh. Kill me now."

But I didn't.

german

10:20 a.m.

In the spirit of European whatsit and also because I had finished painting my nails, I asked Herr Kamyer what was German for snogging. He went amazingly dithery and red. At first he pretended not to know what snogging meant, but when Rosie and Jools started puckering up and blowing kisses at him he got the message. Anyway, it's called *frontal knutschen*.

As we left class I said to Rosie, "I rest my case vis-à-vis the German people. I will never *knutsch* any of them."

french

1:30 p.m.

When Jackie Bummer went up to collect her homework(!) she stood so close to Henri that she was practically resting her nunga-nungas on his head. If he had had the misfortune to have seen her in her sports knickers as I have, he would have been away laughing on a fast camel. (Or as Henri would say, "away laughing on *le vite* camel.")

Uh-oh, I am thinking about Dave the Laugh again. *Merde.*

6:00 p.m.

Robbie phoned to say he really likes me. (Yeah!!!) He is going down to London (Booo!) for his meeting vis-à-vis becoming a HUGE star. (Hurrah!)

A HUGE star with a really great girlfriend.

6:10 p.m.

I went into the kitchen to have a cheesy snack to celebrate. Angus was having a zizz in his basket. Even though he is no longer fully intact trouser snake–wise he is very cheerful. He was purring like a bulldozer. When I gave him one of his kitty treats he almost decapitated my hand. Libby wanted a kitty treat as well. I said, "They are not for human beings, Libby."

"I like human beans."

"Yes but—"

"Give me human beans as well!!!!"

I had to give her one. Then the Loonleader came in and said, "Who are all these mystery boys then that keep phoning you?"

I went "Hnyunk" which in anybody's except an absolute fool's language means, "It is none of your business, and I will be sick on your slippers if you go on."

Vati, of course, didn't get it. He raved on. "Why don't you bring them round here for us to meet?" On and on and ON about it.

I said, "As I have said many, many times, I have to be going now."

my bedroom

8:00 p.m.

Everyone has gone out. I've got so much homework and so on it will be a relief to really get down to it.

8:05 p.m.

Oh Blimey O'Reilly's pantyhose . . . what is the point of Shakespeare? I know he is a genius and so on, but he does rave on. *What light doth through yonder window break?*

It's the bloody moon, for God's sake, Will, get a grip!!

Phoned Rosie. "The Sex God has to go to London to see the record company people and discuss making an album. I don't mean to boast but I have to. . . . Not only am I the girlfriend of a Sex God, I am now going to be fantastically rich."

"Fab. Groovesville, Arizona. Are you going to be living in an all-white penthouse with parrots?"

Sometimes I really worry about my friends. Parrots?

Then I could hear in the background, "Parrots? Parrots? Oh *ja*." Sven seemed really interested in these bloody parrots, my new flatmates.

Rosie said, "Hang on a minute."

Her massive Norwegian boyfriend always seems to be round her house: that is because she has very, very nice parents who go out a lot. I could hear kissing noises and giggling and a sort of Norwegian parrot thing.

When she came back Rosie said, "Sven says, Can we come and live with you in your groovy London pad?"

"No."

"Fair enough."

11:00 p.m.

I won't let my newfound happiness with a famous popstar spoil me though, and I definitely want my own career. Using one of my many talents. Hmmm . . . What career combines being able to apply makeup with innovative trouser snake dancing?

I could be a heavily made-up girl backup dancer!

wednesday november 10th
biology

1:30 p.m.

I can do a magnificent impression of a bolus of food being passed along the alimentary canal. Mrs. Hawkins said it was "terrifyingly realistic." So I'll probably get top marks in blodge and become, erm, what is it you become when you do biology? . . . A bloke with a beard ferretting round in swamps. Maybe I'll stick with the backup dancer idea.

10:00 p.m.

I had to go to bed because Vati was singing "I Will Always Love Youuuuuuuuuuuuuuuuuuuuuuuuuuuuuuuuuuuuuuuuuuuuuuuuuu" by Whitney Useless.

11:00 p.m.

Just nodding off when I heard this noise at my window like pebbles being thrown against it. Angus has made a startling recovery, but surely even he hadn't learnt how to throw pebbles. I opened the window and looked out, and there below me was the Sex God!! Aahhhhh. He blew me a kiss when I opened the window, and he said, "Come down."

I put on my coat over my jimjams and had just a second to remember my emergency Sex God drill—lip gloss, comb idiot hair, suck in nostrils—before I crept downstairs and opened the door. The olds were all still up in the front room, singing the national anthem, only to a reggae beat. . . . I suspect a few barrels of Vino Tinto had been drunk.

Robbie gave me a really dreamy long kiss when I came out. I whispered, "Brrr, it's very nippy noodles, isn't it?"

Robbie looked at me like I was half insane (and half bonkers). Which I am so sure he is not wrong there. SHUT UP, BRAIN!!!!

in bed
midnight
He has gone.

    To London.

    Without me.

thursday november 11th
8:30 a.m.
Still, life carries on. Exams to be examined. Serious things to be thingied.

Today we have decided on Operation La Belle France.

The whole gang went to school wearing our berets like *les françaises* and also with our collars on our coats turned up. Rosie even brought a bunch of onions for Henri, which in my personal opinion is taking things just that little bit too far. He was all groovy and smiley and said, "*Merci, mademoiselle*, I will make the *delicieusement soupe a l'oignon ce soir* and I will think of you when I eat it."

Which is a plus and a minus in my book. *Très bon* to be thought of by Henri but not so *bon* to be associated with onions. He said it all in *la française* and I knew what he meant. I smiled at him to let him know that I knew what it meant.

11:00 a.m.

The French test didn't seem all that difficult.

We have got Henri fever. Badly. All this morning we wandered round going "Haw he haw he haw" in a French accent.

p.e.

1:30 p.m.

I think even Miss Stamp might be on the turn because of Henri. I could have sworn she has had a shave.

break

2:30 p.m.

Ellen and me were sitting on the radiator near the vending machine. In these cold autumn days it's quite pleasant having toastie knickers. I said to Ellen with great casualosity, "How's it going with you and Dave the Laugh?"

She said, "Quite cool."

What does that mean? I tell you what it means: it means that he hasn't told her about our accidental snog.

I may live to snog another day.

saturday november 13th

11:00 a.m.

Very, very bad Sex God withdrawal.

midday

Even though I am not in the mood for shopping

because I am so sad and aloney I forced myself to ask Mum for a fiver and made an effort to go out. Rosie, Jools, Ellen and Jas and me met at Luigi's as normal and then went off to Miss Selfridge. On the way there we had to go through the town center and we were just walking along all linked up when we saw Dave the Laugh with Rollo and a couple of other mates. Uh-oh.

Dave the Laugh said, "Hi, dream chicks."

He is a very fit-looking boy. It's funny that even though, of course, I am really sorry (honestly, Jesus) about the red-bottom business, it is always nice to see him. I never feel like such a stupid loon round him as I do with the Sex God. We were close to Jennings the greengrocer's, where Tom works, so Jas HAD to pop in to see her so-called boyfriend.

I said, "Ask him if he has got any firm legumes." But she didn't pay any attention to me.

Ellen was being really girlie round Dave and flicking her hair about. They were chatting and I was pretending to be looking at things with Rosie. But really I wanted to know what Dave the L was saying to Ellen. I still didn't know if they were official snogging partners.

The lads went off and Dave gave Ellen a little kiss on her cheek.

It made me feel a bit funny, actually. I don't know why.

3:00 p.m.

Ellen was all stupid for the rest of the afternoon. She is going to the flicks tonight, so she said she had to go home to get ready. I said to Rosie, "So are they an item then?"

Rosie said, "I know that she thinks he's really cool, but she won't tell me what number they have got up to. She says it's private."

I said, "That's pathetic."

And Rosie said, "I know, but I'll keep my beadies on them tonight at the cinema and see if I can tell."

It turns out that everyone—Jas and Tom, Rosie and Sven, Ellen and Dave, Jools and Rollo and a few more couples—are all going out together tonight. Everyone, that is, besides me.

Merde.

I am a goosegog in my own country.

3:30 p.m.

Phoned Jas.

"I am a goosegog in my own country."

"Well, come along tonight then."

"I can't. You'll all be having a snogging fest. Don't worry. I'll just stay in whilst my best mates all go out together."

She said, "Oh, OK then. See you later."

Charming. And typico.

8:00 p.m.

SG phoned. Oooohhhhh. The record company wants to sign them up!!! They are going along to this big music industry party tonight at some trendy club.

midnight

I am a pop widow.

sunday november 14th
lunchtime

1:10 p.m.

Phoned Rosie. She said, "*Bonjour, ma petite* pal."

"What are you doing?"

"Having an Abba afternoon. I am wearing my

mum's old crochet bikini and . . . Sven! Careful of that glass chandelier!!"

In the background I could hear all this clattering and, "Oh *ja*, oh *ja*, oh *ja*!"

I said, "What is Sven doing?"

"He's juggling."

Of course he was. Why do I ask?

2:00 p.m.

Jas is swotting with her boyfriend AGAIN.

No one will play with me. They are all doing their homework. Huh.

8:00 p.m

Alarmingly, I found myself in my room doing some French homework!!! Even Dad came to the door to look. This is a new sign of my maturiosity. Also, I must make sure I can order things in Paris when I am traveling over there with the band. I would feel like a fool if I didn't even know how to order mascara.

9:00 p.m.

The evening did end on a high note though. When I was in the kitchen making myself milky pops for my restless urges, Vati was hanging round in there. Talking to me and asking me stuff. I told him all about the SG and Dave the L (not). Then he said, "I think that Angus has definitely calmed down."

At that moment Angus came in through the cat flap in what can only be described as a bird's nest hat.

I love him, I love him!!!

monday november 15th
french
1:30 p.m.

Hmmm. Henri gave us back our test papers and I had come top!!! All the ace crew looked at me in amazement.

Jools said, "*Sacré* bloody *bleu*."

But Henri gave me a really dishy smile. He said, "This is vair, vair well done, m'mselle."

Blimey O'Reilly's trousers. He is quite literally GORGEOUS! If I wasn't the girlfriend of a Sex God and also dying to go to the piddly diddly department I would have snogged him on the spot.

break

2:30 p.m.

As we left French and went to the canteen Henri was ahead of us. He has got excellent bottomosity. Herr Kamyer came bounding and dithering along the corridor. He looked delighted to see Henri.

"*Guten tag*, Henri. Vould you like a cup of coffee?" And they went off to the staff room.

I said, "Herr Kamyer is making an absolute arse of himself, isn't he? Drooling around after Henri. Like a homosexualist."

Jas went all politically correct. "Well, there is nothing wrong with that. He might be gay, you know. He might be looking for happiness with the right man."

"Jas, don't be ridiculous. He wears tartan socks."

at home

4:30 p.m.

Yesss!!! I came top in French! That will teach Madame Slack. In fact, I will tell her when she gets back, possibly in French, that instead of the stick she should have used *le* carrot. Like Henri. Ooer.

7:00 p.m.

To celebrate Vati's fabulous new job at the waterworks (!), I was forced to go out to a family meal at Pizza Express. Libby brought scuba-diving Barbie, Pantalitzer, Charlie Horse and a Pingu comic, so we had to have a table for eight because she wanted them all to have seats of their own. (Yes, even the comic). She tried to order them their own pizzas as well but Vati put his foot down with a firm hand. Even when she cried real tears. He said, "There are children starving in Africa."

I nearly said, Well, why don't you send your bottom off to them? That should keep them going through the winter."

But I didn't want to spoil a beautiful evening.

10:00 p.m.

Sex God phoned. Yummmmmm!

He is relanding on Sunday. Actually he is coming back on Saturday and going to a family party: it's his mum's birthday. Jas is going with Tom. I sort of waited for him to ask me.

He said, "It would be great if you could come, Georgia, but maybe we should wait and introduce you to them first before you just turn up? What do you think?"

"Er . . ."

midnight

What do I think? What does he mean, what do I think? How should I know? If anyone knows what I think it won't be me. I, of course, will be the last to know. Hmmm, I wish me and the Sex God could see more of each other and you know, do normal things like . . . Abba afternoons . . . and . . . snogging. And trouser snake dancing. And so on.

Maybe when we live in our penthouse flat in London.

1:00 a.m.

How many hours is it till the Sex God returns?

Twenty-four times five plus the difference between . . . oh God. I don't know. I can't do figures in my head very well. There are too many other really important things in there taking up the space. Fashion tips and so on.

tuesday november 16th
maths
2:45 p.m.

Didn't those Greek-type people have anything to do but loll round in baths going "Eureka"!!? And also I'll just say this about Pythagoras: didn't he have any mates? Mates that would say, "Hey, Pythy baby . . . SHUT UP!!!!"

4:01 p.m.

We were just pinning on our ears to do glove animal on the way home when we spotted Dave the Laugh and Rollo and Steve and a few others, hanging round . . . Ooer. Lad alert, lad alert!!! Damn, I didn't have any lippy on, but at least I could quickly rip my ears off. Ellen was patheticisimus—she ran back into the cloakroom, going, "Oops, forgot my fags!"

Oh yeah!

She came out five minutes later with just the merest hint of makeup on—lip gloss, concealer, glossy eyeshadow, mascara . . . skirt rolled over, hair tousled . . . really natural.

I said, "Found your fags then?" But she didn't get it.

Dave is cool-looking. In a someone-else's-boyfriend sort of a way. He gave Ellen a kiss on the cheek. Then he looked at me. I hadn't noticed how long his eyelashes are before. Probably because he had been a Red Herring and then he had been wearing a big red false nose. He said, "Hi, Georgia. Still grooving?"

I said, "Yeah, grooving like two grooving . . . er . . . groovers."

And he laughed.

Ellen said, "Are you walking home?" And we all set off together.

Dave has been banned from school for a week. Hmm . . . my kind of guy. I asked him why.

"Well, you know that methylated spirit just burns and doesn't burn anything else?"

Ellen (space rocket scientist—not) said, "Oh yeah. It's to do with its low combustion point, isn't it?"

And she was being all girlie and sort of hanging on his arm. I wondered what number they had got up to. Rosie said she thought number five (open-mouth kissing). She couldn't really tell in the dark at the cinema. Also, had he done that nip libbling thing? Shut up. Shut up. Remember I am the girlfriend of a Sex God.

Dave said, "Anyway, in science I put some meths on my hand and set fire to it. Then when Mr. Martin asked a question I put up my hand. On fire. It was hilarious in the extreme, even if I do say so myself. Which I just did, because I heard myself."

It really made me laugh.

Rosie has asked them all to come over to her house on Saturday because her parents are out for the night. After we split up at the bottom of the hill, I said, "It was a laugh about the hand-on-fire thing, wasn't it?"

And Ellen said, "Don't you think it was a bit dangerous?"

I have my doubts whether she is quite laugh enough for Dave the Laugh.

teatime

Vati was grumbling and raving on for England because the milkman won't deliver milk to us anymore. He says that Angus stalks him. Oh honestly, people are so weedy. I had more important things to think about than the milkman's trousers, believe me.

When Dad had gone off to visit the permanently

insane (Uncle Eddie), I said to Mum, "Mum, you know I don't really like talking about this sort of thing, but, well . . . did you ever, you know, when you were a teenager, did you ever two-time anyone?"

"Oh yes."

"How did you feel?"

"Great."

"Great?!"

"Yes."

"You didn't feel guilty then?"

"No."

"Well, you should have."

"Well, I didn't."

You see what I am up against.

thursday november 18th
physics
10:20 a.m.

The Bummer Twins cut off half Nauseating P. Green's tie. I tried to cheer her up. I had to even pretend that I was glad she had named one of Hammy's children after me. That is what I am like. I may have red bottomosity, but I also have wisdomosity and self-sacrificiosity. Which is not easy to say.

lunchtime

Nippy noodles. I'm sure Elvis Attwood turns the heating down when it gets cold. We all huddled on the radiator in the Science block. We were safe because it was Tragic Kate and Melanie Griffiths on prefect duty and neither of them are in peak physical condition (due to extreme breastiness in Melanie's case and general fatness in Kate's). They can never be arsed to check beyond the second floor. If Wet Lindsay or Hawkeye is on duty there is quite literally no hiding place. Once I had the unfortunate experience of hiding in the loo with my legs up against the door, pretending there was no one in there (as you do). Then, when I thought it was all clear, I looked down to see Hawkeye's beady eyes looking up at me from underneath the door. Scary bananas.

It's the dreaded sex and relationship lecture from Miss Wilson tomorrow. I said, "I will be wearing my earplugs. I cannot bear to have grown-ups discuss sex. It's unnatural."

Jas said, "Haven't your mum and dad told you the facts of life thing?"

I looked at her. "Erlack."

Actually, Mutti did once ramble on about eggs

and ovaries when my period started. I didn't happen to have my earplugs with me so I had to hum a little tune in my head.

I said to the gang, "All we can hope for is that we get some free sanitary towels."

Jas (the sanitary wear expert) said, "Don't you use tampons? They're so much more convenient. Why don't you use them?"

Resisting my natural urge to shove her off the radiator I explained, "Because if I use them, Libby finds them, takes them out of their little holder and calls them 'Georgia's mice.' She trails them around for Angus to hunt. You have no idea what it is like in my house."

special assembly
3:40 p.m.
Slim was beyond the Valley of the Jelloid. Mr. Attwood caught the Bummer Twins in his hut snogging with the two window cleaners who came to do the Science block windows!!!

Slim said it was "disgraceful behavior."

I don't know why she has got her gigantic knickers in such a twist. She is the one, after all, who is encouraging us to be interested in sex by making us go to lectures on it. But you cannot reason with multiple chin personalities.

Anyway, on the plus side, the Bummers are banned for two weeks and may actually be expelled. Oh dear. How sad. Never mind.

friday november 19th
11:00 a.m.

Another reprimand! Just because Hawkeye heard me say "*Schiessenhausen*" when I tripped over Jas's haversack strap. *Gott in Himmel*, you can't even say lavatory in German without some fascist taking offense.

r.e.
1:30 p.m.

Sex and relationship talk. We all tried to get as far to the back of the classroom as we possibly could.

It was EXCRUCIATING! First of all, we were shown a film about ovaries and sperm and so on, which was enough to put you off sex for life. Additionally the woman in the film looked like Meat Loaf. It was really giving me the mega droop.

To pass the idle hours Rosie sent round a note:

To whom it may concern.
You have to choose one of these.
Which would you rather?
1. Elvis Attwood gets to number seven with
you. Heavy tongues are involved. He is in
the nuddy-pants.
or
2. No snogging ever again.
Pass it on.

And we all had to put 1 or 2. Everyone put 2. The thought of Elvis getting to number seven (upper body fondling—outdoors) has made my nunga-nungas quiver.

The next note was:

Which would you rather?
1. Miss Stamp rubs you down with a towel
in the showers.
or
2. No snogging ever again.

I was very alarmed to see that Jas put number 1.

break

I said to Jas, "What kind of snacks have you got, lezzie?"

I can't bear to think about the second half of the sex and relationship lecture given by the saddest, most unlikely person ever to have sex or a relationship, Miss Wilson. I personally think that if you can't even put your tights on properly you are not likely to be tiptop in the snogging department. She raved and stuttered on about the "beauty of a fulfilling and caring relationship with someone you love."

Heavens to Betsy. Rosie colored all her teeth black with her fibertip pen which was very funny. (And much funnier later when she couldn't get it off.)

In the end Miss Wilson gave us each an egg. Cheers. Just what I've always wanted. What in the name of Lucifer is she on about? We have to take care of the egg and look after it and treat it like a baby. It is supposed to teach us about caring and nurturing.

It is totally sad and useless and *merde*.

8:30 p.m.

I annoyed Vati by telling him that the program he was watching on TV was unsuitable for my egg. Which by the way I have dressed in an old bootie of Libby's.

I think I may very well be an unusually good mother.

*Egg*cellent, in fact.

saturday november 20th

2:45 p.m.

Saturday night is party night.

I've asked Mum to baby-sit my egg. It will make a change for her to nurture her caring skills.

The ace gang is going to be there. (Well, apart from Jas, who is going to her so-called boyfriend's house to celebrate with her so-called boyfriend's parents.) Robbie said he would come round to Rosie's if he could after the family do. I feel sheer desperadoes to see him again. It's been ages since I saw him. Oh well. I wonder who will turn up tonight? Rosie and Sven, of course; Mabs and Steve, Jools and Rollo, Ellen and Dave the Laugh . . . Sara, Patty and me . . . and maybe some of Dave the Laugh's mates.

I'm sort of looking forward to it. It will take my mind off my jelloidness about the SG. Even though I will be, as per usual, the goosegog in the manger.

rosie's house

8:20 p.m.

Sven opened the door wearing a Durex on his head like a hat . . . er . . .

"'Ello, welcome to the fish party!"

What was he going on about?

When we went into the living room it was all full of netting and paper fish hanging up.

Rosie was wearing a really crap mermaid's outfit (her legs down one leg of her blue trousers and hobbling around). She said, "Cod evening."

Good grief.

Actually it was quite funny. There were fish-fingers as snacks. Dave the Laugh arrived with his mates. Ellen was really giddy, but I was cool as a mackerel. Sven said, "Let's dance," and we had to dance to fish-type music. Like the music from *Jaws*. And *Titanic*. Like fish. Which is not as easy as you would think because fish aren't big dancers. Dave was making me laugh because he really did look like a fish dancing! He even said,

"This dancing is playing haddock with my jeans."

Then we played sardines—well, we played Sven's version of it, which meant that essentially we all got into the wardrobe and some people snogged. Although I am not naming names. But it was Rollo and Jools, and Sven and Rosie. I was a bit too close to Dave the Laugh for my liking. He had to put his arm round me to stop falling over. It almost made me pucker up in the dark. . . .

Oh, stop it, stop it. I can feel my bottom getting redder and redder and bigger. I must not, MUST NOT get the big red bottom.

9:20 p.m.

Back in the living room the gang were playing True, Dare, Kiss or Promise. Then the doorbell rang. It was Mrs. Big Knickers herself and Tom. No Sex God though. I said to Jas confidentially, "Where is Robbie?"

"Who?"

God, she is annoying. She went off to help herself to snacks. I followed her and said, "Jas, what did he say?"

Then in front of the whole room she said, "You know when you did ear snogging with him? Well, what number is that officially?"

What is the matter with her?!! If anyone wants to know anything about my life all they have to do is to tune into Radio Jas.

9:30 p.m.

Hahahaha. Jas got "Dare" from me and I dared her to fill her knickers up with all the legumes in the vegetable basket. She was grumbling but in the end she had to do it and she went off to the kitchen.

I almost died with laughing when she came back. She had two pounds of potatoes, four carrots and a Swede down her knicknacks. And they were not full!!!

Rosie had to tell the truth about what number she and Sven had got up to. It was . . . eight!!!! They had got up to upper body fondling—indoors. Honestly!!! It gave me quite a turn. Rosie wasn't a bit embarrassed or anything. Then Steve got "Dare" and had to eat a raw onion.

Uh-oh, my turn.

Jas got her own back for the vegetable knicker extravaganza in a really horrible way. I got "True," and she said, "Do you fancy anyone besides the Sex God?"

Dave the Laugh looked at me. Everyone looked at me. What was I? A looking-at thing?

I said, "Er . . . well, I quite fancy . . . er, Henri." Phew.

That got them talking about Henri and his trousers. The game went on and then . . . Dave the Laugh got "Kiss." Jools said, "OK, Dave, you have to kiss . . ."

Ellen went all pink and incredibly girlish. But then Jools said, "You have to kiss . . . Georgia. . . ."

Why did she say that? What did she know? Was my big red bottom showing under my skirt????

Whilst everyone went "Snog, snog, snog!", I went into the kitchen to get myself a drink.

I was in a state of confusiosity. I wish I knew what I wanted. I wanted everything.

I wanted the Sex God and Dave the Laugh, and also possibly Henri.

Good Lord. I really was a nymphowhatsit.

That is when Dave the Laugh came out.

"Georgia."

"What?"

"You owe me a snog."

Oh God's pajamas!!! He was my best pal's

boyfriend. I was the girlfriend of a Sex God.

I would just have to say "No, Dave, the game is over."

And that is when I accidentally snogged him. AGAIN!!!

Oh, my lips had no discipline!! They were bad, bad lips!!! Then he stopped, mid–nip libbling, and said, "Georgia, we shouldn't be doing this."

That was what I was going to say!

He said, "Look, I really, really like you. I always have, you know that. But I am not an idiot, and, you know, other girls like me. They are only human; you have seen my dancing. . . ."

That made me laugh even amidst the drama-tosity.

He went on, because I seemed to be paralyzed from the nose downwards. Well, from the neck upwards and the nose downwards: "You have to choose. You go for a Sex God or you go for me, who really likes you and who you could have a great time with."

Then he gave me a little soft kiss on the mouth and went back into the living room.

midnight

In my bed. With my egg child tucked up next to me.

I am beyond the Valley of the Confused and treading lightly in the Universe of the Severely Deranged. *Sacré* bloody *bleu*. I am supposed to be thinking about makeup and my nunga-nungas. Not life-changing decisions. And egg babies. Why can't I just be left alone, why do I have to care about everything? I'm only fourteen. I only just snogged someone a few months ago and now I am practically married and have an egg child.

Jas hasn't got red-bottomosity, so it's all very well for her to be boring.

But my bottom demands to be heard.

1:00 a.m.

Oh *sacré* bloody *bleu*. I can't sleep.

Sex God or the Laugh?

Or both.

1:15 a.m.

Jelloid knickers or strange dancing?

Ear snogging or nip libbling?

It is a stark choice.

1:20 a.m.

I wonder what sort of snogging Henri does. Perhaps *les français* do other things that are not on the English snogging scale. Nose libbling, *peut-être*. That might be quite nice.

1:30 a.m

Nose libbling???!!!!

What am I talking about???!!!!

sunday november 21st
at breakfast

10:45 a.m.

I think I'm going mad. I feel so bonkers that at this rate I might be driven to ask advice from my mutti. I went into the kitchen and I began to say "Mutti, I have a . . ." but then I was so astonished I forgot what I was going to say. For once in her life, Mum had actually made breakfast for me and Libbs. Boiled eggs and soldiers. Amazing. And she was practically fully dressed. It was almost like being in a real family. Possibly. I tapped the top of my egg and scooped a bit out, and Mum said, "Georgia, don't let Libby take eggs in your bed. I found that one on your pillow."

I was eating my child.

That is the kind of person I have become.

A red-bottomed child eater.

What could be worse than that?

Then Vati came bursting through the door and said, "Christ on a bike . . . Naomi is pregnant!!!"

in my room

midday

In my bed of pain.

I can still see the little indent in the pillow where my egg child spent so many happy hours.

Who is Naomi pregnant by?

Have Angus's missing addendums made a surprise reappearance? Or has he been cuckolded by the little minx? Perhaps Vati is right that all women are fickle. My own mutti said she liked being a double dater. She thrust her nungas at Dr. Clooney. And now Naomi has allowed her girlie parts to flow free and wild. She has displayed appalling red-bottomosity.

But how can I point the fingers of shame? I am just the same.

No, I am worse.

Much, much worse.

I am a red-bottomed child eater.

Oh *merde*.

The End

4:00 p.m.

However, on the bright side—God wouldn't have made me have a red bottom in the first place unless he was trying to tell me something. He is, as we all know, impotent. (Or do I mean omnipotent? I don't know, but anyway he is some kind of potent.) Perhaps he is saying, "Go forth, Georgia, and use your red bottom wisely."

Hmmmm. So maybe I could have the Sex God AND Dave the Laugh?

And perhaps for diplomatic world relationship type stuff Henri as well?

Cor, it's all a go!!!

Georgia's Glossary

articles • (as in "You two articles get in here now!") A term of disdain used by so-called grown-ups. Because of their disdain of you they no longer see you as a human being but merely as a thing, an article.

backup dancer • This is like a backup singer, only it is dancing. At the back. Do you get it?

balaclava • This is from the Crimean War when our great-great-grannies spent all their time knitting hats to keep the English soldiers warm in the very, very cold Baltic. A balaclava covers everything apart from your eyes. It is like a big sock with a hole in it. Which just goes to show what really crap knitters our great-great-grannies were.

bangers • Firecrackers. Fireworks that just explode with a big bang. That's it. No pretty whooshing or stars or rocketing up into the sky. Bangers just bang. Boy fireworks. Boys are truly weird.

Blimey O'Reilly • (as in "Blimey O'Reilly's trousers") This is an Irish expression of disbelief and shock. Maybe Blimey O'Reilly was a famous Irish bloke who had extravagantly big trousers. We may never know the truth. The fact is, whoever he is, what you need to know is that a) it's Irish and b) it is Irish. I rest my case.

blodge • Biology. Like geoggers—geography—or Froggie—French.

Boots • A large drugstore chain selling mostly cosmetics.

David Ginola • A spectacularly good-looking French football player who plays in England. He has very long hair that he conditions and swishes round. He also carries a handbag. In any other circumstances he would definitely be a homosexualist. However, we must remember he is French.

DIY • Quite literally "Do It Yourself!" Rude when you think about it. Instead of getting someone competent to do things around the house (you know, like a trained electrician or a builder or a plumber), some vatis choose to DIY. Always with disastrous results. (For example, my bedroom ceiling has footprints in it because my vati decided he would go up on the roof and replace a few tiles. Hopeless.)

duffing up • Duffing up is the female equivalent of beating up. It is not so violent and usually involves a lot of pushing with the occasional pinch.

Durex • Oh do I really have to go into this? Honestly, everyone is OBSESSED with sex. A Durex is a . . . oh, you know. Yes, you do. It's a thingy. A boy thingy. Now do you get it? Oh very well, you asked me . . . a Durex is a condom. See. I knew you wouldn't like it if I told you.

fringe • Goofy short bit of hair that comes down to your eyebrows. Someone told me that American-type people call them "bangs" but this is so ridiculously strange that it's not worth thinking about. Some people can look very stylish with a fringe (i.e., me) while others look goofy (Jas). The Beatles started it apparently. One of them had a German girlfriend, and she cut their hair with a pudding bowl and the rest is history.

ginger nob • Someone with red hair. Red hair in England is a sign of lunacy. This stems from Henry VIII, who had red hair and also cut people's heads off. A lot. For a laugh.

goosegog • Gooseberry. I know you are looking all quizzical now. OK. If there are two people and they want to snog and you keep hanging about saying "Do you fancy some chewing gum?" or "Have you seen my interesting new socks?" you are a gooseberry. Or for short a goosegog, i.e., someone who nobody wants around.

goss • Gossip. Not to be confused with guss (gusset).

gyp • Who knows what this means? It's just something you say, like "Gadzooks!" Essentially *gyp* means "a pain." Elvis Attwood says I give him gyp. He also says his old war wound gives him gyp as well.

haggis • Something else that the Jock McThicks have made up to horrify the civilized world. It is a pudding made out of stuffed sheep's stomach.

Irn-bru • Pronounced "iron broo."
   A disgusting drink made from sugar and old socks. Probably. People in Och Aye land think it is yummy scrumbos.

Jammy Dodger • Biscuit with jam in it. Very nutritious (ish).

Jock McThick • Is a generic term for anyone from Scotland that you can't be bothered to find out the name of. Can also be called Jock McTavish. Ditto French people (Jacques Lefrog) or German (Hans Lederhosen).

Kiwi-a-gogo land • New Zealand. "A-gogo land" can be used to liven up the otherwise really boring names of other countries. America, for instance, is Hamburger-a-gogo land. Mexico is Mariachi-a-gogo land and France is Frogs'-legs-a-gogo land. This is from that very famous joke told every Christmas by the elderly mad (Grandad). Oh, very well, I'll tell you it.

A man goes into a French restaurant and says to the French waiter, "Have you got frogs' legs?"

The waiter says, *"Oui, monsieur."*

And the man says, "Well, hop off and get me a sandwich then."

This should give you some idea of what our Christmases are like.

la mouche • Or possibly *le mouche*. This, as everyone who is *très bon* at *le français* (i.e., *moi*) knows, means "the fly."

loo • Lavatory. In America they say "rest room," which is funny, as I never feel like having a rest when I go to the lavatory.

lurgy • Is when you feel icky-poo. Please tell me that you know what *icky-poo* means. Oh good Lord. It means "poorly." Lurgy is like a bug. An illness bug. Ergo, tummy lurgy = stomach bug.

milky pops • A hot milk drink usually drunk by children to calm them down at night. You'd have to give it intravenously to Libby to calm her down. Or alternatively make the hot drink, put it in Libby's cup and then hit her over the head with it.

Miss Selfridge • A store where teenage girls go and buy clothes.

naff • Unbearably and embarrassingly out of fashion and nerdy. Naff things are: Parents dancing to "modern" music, blue eyeshadow, blokes who wear socks with sandals, pigtails. You know what I mean.

nervy spaz • Nervous spasm. Nearly the same as a nervy b. (nervous breakdown) or an F.T. (funny turn), only more spectacular on the physical side.

nippy noodles • Instead of saying "Good heavens, it's quite cold this morning," you say "Cor—nippy noodles!!" English is an exciting and growing language. It is. Believe me. Just leave it at that. Accept it.

nuddy-pants • Quite literally nude-colored pants, and you know what nude-colored pants are? They are no pants. So if you are in your nuddy-pants you are in your no pants, i.e., you are naked.

Number 10 • Number 10 Downing Street in London, where the Prime Minister lolls around.

nunga-nungas • Basoomas. Girl's breasty business. Ellen's brother calls them nunga-nungas because he says that if you get hold of a girl's breast and pull it out and then let it go—it goes *nunga-nunga-nunga*. As I have said many, many times with great wisdomosity, there is something really wrong with boys.

Och Aye land • Scotland. Land of the Braves. Or is that Indiana? I don't know, and I know I should because we are, after all, all human beings under our skins. But I still don't care.

Pantalitzer • A terrifying Czech-made doll that sadistic parents (my vati) buy for their children, presumably to teach them early on about the horror of life. Essentially the Pantalitzer doll has a weird plastic face with a horrible fixed smile. The rest of Pantalitzer is a sort of cloth bag with hard plastic hands on each side like steel forks.

I don't know if I have mentioned this before, but I am not reassured that Eastern Europeans really know how to have a laugh.

pantibus • Latin for pants. Possibly. Who cares? It is a dead language. Who is going to complain if it isn't Latin for pants—Romulus and Remus?

pensioner • In England we give very old people some money so that they can buy thick spectacles and snug incontinent pants and biscuits. This is called their pension money.

piggies • Pigtails. Or "bunches," I think you call them. Like two little side ponytails in your hair. Only we think they look like pigtails. English people are obsessed with pigs; that is our strange beauty.

pingy pongoes • A very bad smell. Usually to do with farting.

porkies • Amusing (ish) Cockney rhyming slang. Pork pies = lies. Which is of course shortened to porkies. Oh, that isn't shorter, is it? Well, you can't have everything.

prat • A prat is a gormless oik. You make a prat of yourself by mistakenly putting both legs down one knicker leg or by playing air guitar at pop concerts.

pushbike • A pedal cycle, bicycle. Nothing will make me go on a bicycle again since my skirt got caught in the spokes of the back wheel and my panties were exposed.

rate • To fancy someone. Like I fancy (or rate) the Sex God. And I certainly *do* fancy the SG as anyone with the brains of an earwig (i.e., not Jas) would know by now. Phew—even writing about him in the glossary has made me go all jelloid. And stupidoid.

R.E. • Religious education.

Sellotape • Sellotape is a clear sticky tape. Usually used for sticking bits of paper to other bits of paper but can be used for sticking hair down to make it flat. (Once I used it for sticking Jas's mouth shut when she had hiccups. I thought it might cure them. It didn't, but it was quite funny, anyway.)

snogging • Kissing.

soldiers • Toast cut into narrow strips and then dipped into your boiled egg. It's an Olde-English-nursery-rhyme thing. Before you ask, no, toast dipped in egg does not look like a soldier. Obviously. Soldiers are not generally an inch high and covered in butter. As I have told you, we English are a mystery even to ourselves.

sporrans • Ah, I'm glad you asked me about this because it lets me illustrate my huge knowledgosity about Och Aye land. Sporrans are bits of old sheep that Scotsmen wear over their kilts, at the front, like little furry aprons. Please don't ask me why. I feel a nervy spaz coming on.

swot • A person who has no life and as a substitute has to read books and learn things for school. Also anyone who does their homework on time.

tart • A girl who is a bit on the common side. This is a tricky one, actually, because if I wear a very short skirt I am cool and sexy. However, if Jackie Bummer wears a short skirt it is a) a crime against humanity and b) tarty.

tosser • A special kind of prat. The other way of putting this is "wanker" or "monkey spanker."

weedy • Like a weed. You know like weeds in a garden. Those useless spindly annoying things that get in the way of flowers. A weedy person is like that, useless, spindly and annoying (although obviously not green).

whelk boy • A whelk is a horrible shellfish thing that only the truly mad eat. Slimy and mucuslike. Whelk boy is a boy who kisses like a whelk, i.e., a slimy mucus kisser. Erlack a pongoes.